The Golden Horseshoe II

Search Routes

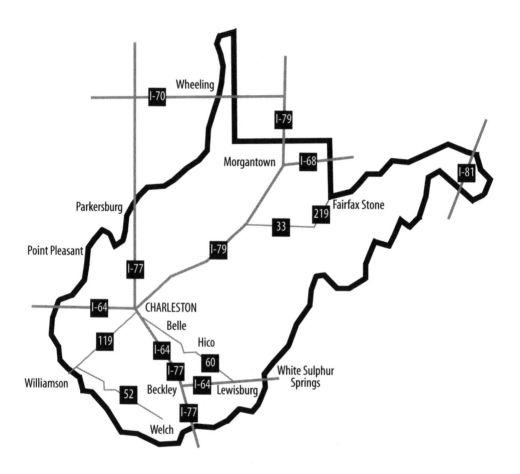

The Golden Horseshoe II

Frances B. Gunter

ELK RIVER
PRESS

Charleston, West Virginia

Elk River Press
Charleston, WV 25302

ISBN-13: 978-0-9710389-2-9
ISBN-10: 0-9710389-2-9
Library of Congress Number: 2003100061

10 9 8 7 6 5 4 3

Printed in United States of America

Book and Cover Design: Mark S. Phillips
Photography: Ron Gunter

Distributed by:

West Virginia Book Company
1125 Central Avenue
Charleston, WV 25302

www.wvbookco.com

Table of Contents

Acknowledgments

I thank the many people who contributed to the writing of this book. My husband Ron served as driver, traveling companion, idea bouncer and photographer. My daughters, Vivian and Ronda, gave suggestions and added bits of humor throughout the writing process. A dear friend Ann Klinestiver acted as editor and computer consultant. Katherine Ferris, historian and portrayer of historical characters, assisted with facts and provided numerous suggestions. Margaret Miller and the teachers of Kanawha County gave me the incentive to continue the fictional travel of teenagers throughout the enchanting state of West Virginia. Many state employees working in the Cultural Center, the Capitol, Tamarack and historical areas provided expertise and valuable time. Members of my church family, Megan Williams along with Joan, Alex, and Kaitlyn McPherson kept me in tune with the student's point of view.

I am also grateful to the teachers in West Virginia. I appreciate their dedication to the profession and the sacrifices they make on behalf of their students. I hope *Golden Horseshoe* I and II will assist you in the classroom.

To those whose contributions I have neglected to note, please accept my apologies. I owe all a great deal.

To Margaret Miller,
with gratitude

Chapter 1

The Search Begins

I can't believe I have left California to come back to West Virginia. I think Mom was glad I decided to come. This time last year she and I were going to Grandma's for Grandpa's funeral. That wasn't any fun at all. Mom's working full time now, and she thinks I shouldn't be at home alone all day. Big deal, if I baby-sit Mrs. Moore's kids, that's OK, but not home alone. Mom is sure hard to figure out. Dad said the trip was up to me and of course my brother David won't even know I'm gone. It was really Chelsea's letter that did it. That crazy golden horseshoe; it's disappeared.

I leaned toward the airplane window and pulled my backpack from the floor onto my lap. I unzipped the front pocket and removed the crumpled letter. I imagined the spinning horseshoe with its diamonds and sapphires and flashing images of mound builders, Dominick Blennerhassett, John Brown, Stonewall Jackson, Sadie McCoy, and the miners on Blair Mountain. The horseshoe seemed to be calling me back as I read.

Ginny—

> *The horseshoe is missing from the pedestal in the*
> *Cultural Center. The glass case was broken and*
> *this note left in its place. Go figure—*

> **Travel toward the mountain peaks, Around the river bends,**
> **Missing treasures are easily found. Allow help from**
> **strangers and friends. Respect your heritage and mountain**
> **lore. Attempt to find clues left by me. Consider the notes**
> **and details. Knowledge is the key.**

1

They're offering a reward. Some people have already started searching. Hurry!

Chelsea

It was last summer that Chelsea and I had found an authentic golden horseshoe in an old trunk at Grandma's house. It was one of the original pendants given to members of a scouting party led by Lieutenant Governor Alexander Spotswood in 1716. The group of approximately sixty men included the first white settlers to view and claim what is now West Virginia. Each time they crossed a mountain or large river, they would name it after King George, drink a toast to his health, and fire a volley of shots. Upon their return to Jamestown, Lt. Governor Spotswood gave each of the gentlemen a miniature jewel encrusted golden horseshoe with the Latin inscription "Sic Juvat Transcendere Montes." Translated, it means, "Thus is was decided to cross the mountains." The Smithsonian Institute in Washington, D.C. has now placed the monetary value of each pendant at one hundred thousand dollars and the historical value of each at five hundred thousand dollars.

As I was wondering about the reward and what I might buy with it, I felt a hand on my shoulder.

"Miss, you'll need to remove your headphones, turn off your CD player, and store your backpack under the seat. We'll be landing in just a few minutes at Yeager Airport," said the stewardess in a dull monotone.

She continued down the aisle making similar comments to other passengers. I folded the letter, shoved it into my backpack, and removed my headphones. I fingered my unruly strawberry blond hair into place and thought about my cousins. Chelsea would be turning sixteen soon and Brad would be a junior at West Virginia University this fall. I wondered if Brad would be staying in Welch, or if he had a summer job. Of course, he would stay at home with his mom and dad, my Aunt Fran, and Uncle Ron. Chelsea would stay with me at Grandma's. Chelsea said this was to keep me company, but I think she was afraid Grandma might begin to like me best.

The scary part of the flight began—a mountaintop landing. I felt the plane dropping fast, almost falling toward the tarmac. Thud! I pushed both feet forward as if I could apply the plane's brakes. The small jet swayed as it began to slow. When the plane finally stopped, a group of visiting

German students sitting in the rear section clapped and cheered. I smiled back at them as I unfastened my seatbelt and heaved my backpack onto my lap. As usual, everyone stood and the rows began to empty, school bus style.

I had just entered Gate A when I spotted Chelsea jumping up and down and waving her arms. Brad, standing quietly beside her, moved a few feet away hoping no one would realize they were together. That would be impossible, since they both had thick, curly dark brown hair, brown eyes, and olive skin tones. I was the one who didn't seem to belong in the family, with my reddish hair, fair complexion and green eyes.

"Ginny, Ginny," shouted Chelsea, "over here."

"I'm coming," I called as I wedged my way past an elderly passenger carrying a huge cat in a cage.

"Boy, am I ever glad you're here. Was the flight OK? Did you think about the note? Do you want to go on to the Cultural Center now?" asked Chelsea as the words tumbled from her mouth.

"I see you haven't changed a bit," I joked as I sat down my backpack to give each of my cousins a hug. "Tell me what you know about the horseshoe and the reward."

We walked past the airport restaurant and entered a corridor with murals of Cranberry Glades and Dolly Sods on opposite walls. We turned sharply right and went into the small baggage claim area with only two luggage conveyors. This was so different from the huge airports in California. As we waited for my two bags and a canvas duffle bag (filled with softballs, gloves, and bats) Chelsea began to bubble with information.

"About three weeks ago, after the Vandalia Gathering, when the Cultural Center opened on Tuesday morning the horseshoe was missing. It had been on display during the Memorial Day weekend and hundreds of people saw it. The guard insisted it was there late Monday night when he made his rounds," Chelsea explained.

"How do we know we can trust the guard?" I asked.

Brad responded, "He was given a lie detector test."

"Yeah," interrupted Chelsea, "he was under suspicion, because there was no sign of a break-in. The police thought it was an inside job."

"Did you leave home for good?" Brad gasped as he used both hands to lift the duffle bag.

"No way," I answered. "You know my dad, he is always after me to practice my batting and hitting. He thinks if I'm good enough, I will get an athletic scholarship to Marshall University."

3

"Please, watch your language." Brad teased, "You know WVU is THE state university."

Chelsea and I grabbed the other two bags and turned left to exit the airport. As we headed toward short-term parking, Chelsea led the way. She stepped from the curb as a small gray pickup truck, blowing its horn, sped by us.

Chelsea jumped back a step and yelled, "Hey, watch where you're going!"

The driver looked into his rear-view mirror and waved.

"Someone you know?" I asked.

"No," she snorted, "and I don't want to know a jerk who drives like that."

"Maybe you should watch where you're going," Brad snapped.

"Just like you to blame me for everything," said Chelsea.

Ignoring her, Brad turned to me and explained, "We thought we would go by the Cultural Center and check out the case and note again. That would give you a chance to see the crime scene."

"Great," I replied.

We reached Brad's white Camry and loaded my gear in the trunk. Chelsea climbed into the back seat, still pouting about Brad's comments, so I got up front with Brad. We made small talk about the flight as the car wound down the curvy road. Within five minutes we entered Greenbrier Street and passed the Capitol and the Cultural Center. We continued past the gated parking lot and turned right into the visitor's lot to park. Chelsea remained quiet as we walked along the brick path toward the Veterans' Memorial on the left and the guardhouse on the right. We stepped onto a curved sidewalk and began to approach the Cultural Center. A sign in front of the building read, Building 9, Culture and History, Library Commission. We started up the steps toward huge glass panels. The massive entry hall, with marble floors and a sparkling chandelier, was decorated with quilts, adorning the walls and suspended from the ceiling.

"Aren't they beautiful?" Chelsea gasped as she turned slowly around to see the colorful display. "Grandma has one like that," she said pointing to a cathedral-patterned quilt.

"I like the geometric one," I replied, "with the deep jewel colors."

Sounding like a typical male, Brad said, "I believe we came to see the broken case and note. You girls can check the quilts out later."

Chelsea gave her brother a fake smile and said, "Oh, lead us on, Great One."

West Virginia Cultural Center

Brad shrugged and moved right, past the reception desk, two display cases, and down the fifty-foot U-shaped ramp into the museum. A Conestoga wagon filled with barrels, trunks, and tools dominated the room. A petite Asian woman and two teenagers, a boy and a girl, were reading the plaque that explained the origin and use of the wagon. Moving around them, we went straight to the pedestal on the left. The broken glass had been removed and yellow police tape circled the column. A sign had been posted on the wall.

> **GOLDEN**
> **HORSESHOE**
> **MISSING**
>
> **REWARD**

I looked at the empty pedestal, "Gee, this doesn't tell you anything. Where did you get the note that you sent me?" I asked Chelsea.

Chelsea replied, "When you register at the desk upstairs, they give you a copy. They can't tell you anything that I haven't already told you. It was missing last Tuesday morning when the Center opened, and the building had been locked. Brad signed the three of us up to help with the search."

"Anyone else searching?" I asked.

Chelsea answered, "Yeah, but they don't tell you who."

"What about the reward?" I questioned.

"They don't tell you how much it is. They just said the Toyota Company was offering a reward as an act of friendship," she explained.

"Speaking of a friendship," I turned Chelsea toward Brad, "I think your brother is interested in one."

We watched as Brad postured around the pretty young Asian woman, telling her all about the wagon. She gazed at him and seemed to forget the two teenagers.

"That's great," Brad said as he looked deep into her eyes. "Maybe we can help each other out. You know, divide up the territory. Let me introduce you to my sister and my cousin."

Brad took the young woman's elbow and maneuvered her toward us. The two teens followed.

"Ginny, Chelsea," began Brad, "this is Sakura, and she goes to Salem-Teikyo University. She's an exchange student. These are two of her students she is tutoring in Japanese this summer."

The lovely young girl smiled sweetly and nodded. She turned toward her students and introduced them. "This is Morgan," she said, gesturing toward the blond girl who appeared to be about Chelsea's age, "and her brother, Erik."

Erik's hazel eyes twinkled and his smile broadened as he reached out to shake our hands. "Are you all searching for the horseshoe, too?" he asked.

"Absolutely," I heard myself answering. "Want to help?"

"That depends on what it involves," Erik replied. "I won't get my driver's license for another eighteen months. If there were any driving involved, Sakura would have to drive. Or, we could ride with you."

"You know Grandmother Becky isn't going to let us ride with strangers," interrupted Morgan.

"That's right," agreed Sakura. "Once we decide who will search where, I will ask Miss Becky's permission."

"Let's go outside to one of the picnic tables and discuss this," Brad said; "maybe we can help each other."

The new threesome agreed and followed Brad as he led them up the ramp. Chelsea and I followed from a distance.

Chelsea whispered under her breath, "What is this, 'Let's help each other bit'"? Have you and Brad lost your mind? We don't need them. I know we can figure this out without any help from those three. Have you thought about the reward?"

I really hadn't. My only thoughts had been about Erik. I explained, "Oh, Chelsea, this will be fun. I just know it. Besides, don't be so greedy."

Chelsea continued to mumble under her breath as we passed the reception desk and went outside toward the picnic table. Brad and his new-found friends were chatting excitedly about the search.

We arrived just as Brad pulled a West Virginia road map from his back pocket. He unfolded the map and placed it in the center of the table. Sakura, Morgan, and Erik slid onto the bench opposite him. Brad remained standing as Chelsea and I took seats beside him.

"Chelsea," said Brad, "get out your copy of the note. Let's see where we should begin."

Chelsea removed the note from her purse and handed it to Brad. He unfolded the note and placed it above the map.

Looking over Brad's shoulder, I read aloud, ***"Travel toward the mountain peaks, around the river bends. . . ."***

"Gee," interrupted Chelsea, "that could be anywhere in the state. Believe me, I know. Where are those maps I had to do last year for Mrs. Klinestiver? There are over thirty rivers in this state. Oh, yeah, mountain peaks, they're everywhere. A lot of help this is."

I remarked, "We have to start somewhere. Besides, the note is the only thing we've got."

"Maybe we should concern ourselves only with the major rivers, or those near mountains," suggested Sakura.

Chelsea rolled her eyes and gave me a nudge with her foot under the table. She said, "The rivers start in the mountains."

"Starting with the major rivers is a good idea," explained Brad, "That would be the Ohio, Monongahela, and Kanawha rivers.

"Missing treasures are easily found. Allow help from strangers and friends."

Morgan chimed in, "Well, that's simple enough. The treasure is the horseshoe and we are the strangers and friends."

"But how do you tie in ***'your heritage and mountain lore'*** with these three rivers?" Erik asked.

In an adult sounding voice, Brad answered, "We'll take each major river and try to pinpoint historic places. Your ***'heritage'*** would relate to your history, right? ***'Mountain lore'*** that's knowledge from our ancestors. So I say we start here."

7

Brad placed his finger at the tip of the northern panhandle and began to trace the Ohio River toward Weirton. "Okay, Miss West Virginia History," he said as he looked at Chelsea, "what do you know about Weirton?"

"Uh, uh, " Chelsea answered, "just move on down the Ohio to Wheeling. It's really important. The state originated there and it served as our capital city twice."

"Anybody got a pencil or pen?" asked Brad.

After fishing in my backpack for a few minutes, I handed Brad a BB&T pen from our bank in California.

"This is a strong possibility," said Brad, drawing a large heavy circle around Wheeling.

All eyes focused on Brad's index finger as he slowly moved it down the map. When he reached Moundsville, I had to speak up. "The mound builders, now that's really history. The old prison might be important, too," I added.

Brad shrugged and said, "Maybe," as he drew a lighter circle around Moundsville.

As he continued along the Ohio, I caught myself holding my breath. There was Parkersburg and Blennerhassett Island. I will never forget Dominic; it wasn't just a dream. I remained quiet as he continued to trace the run of the river.

When he reached Point Pleasant, Erik shouted, "Indians!"

We all jumped as he continued, "Cornstalk, big battles, I've heard that Cornstalk's ghost is still there."

"If there's a ghost, then it's a must for Erik," Sakura remarked as she smiled at her student.

"Why not?" agreed Brad as he circled Point Pleasant in heavy ink. "We might want to check out Huntington. It was an early railroad town," he added, drawing a fainter circle about that city.

"To the Monongahela," Morgan directed as she pointed to Morgantown. "I like that name, Morgantown, don't you?"

"I can't imagine why," Sakura teased.

"There's not much of that river in West Virginia. Most of it flows in Pennsylvania," explained Chelsea.

"Let's skip that one and go on to the Kanawha," I suggested as I pointed to Point Pleasant again.

"Hmm. . .two rivers meet and they form a huge bend. That makes a good argument for searching Point Pleasant," mumbled Brad. He continued to follow the river and his finger stopped in Charleston. "We're here

8

now. Do we make a search?"

"Why not? What time is Grandma expecting us?" I asked.

"We should have a couple of hours to spare before she calls out the police and the dogs," Chelsea joked.

"Yeah, we'll talk about that in just a few minutes," Brad commented as he continued to trace the river.

"Wait a minute," Erik injected. "It doesn't have to be a navigable river. What about the Gauley River, or the New River? They're both in the mountains and they really have the bends. Maybe we could take one of those raft trips. That would be cool."

Everyone agreed as Brad circled the Gauley and New Rivers.

"Maybe, just maybe," Sakura said, "I might be able to convince Miss Becky of that."

"I've been on the New River twice," remarked macho-man Brad as he looked directly at Sakura. "It's safe if you do what the guides tell you to do. I'm sure Mom and Dad will let us go."

Looking at me, Chelsea added, "And if we can go, you can go."

"That's fine with me," I said.

"The higher mountains are in Monongahela Forest," Morgan said as she looked intently at the map. "There are also a lot of rivers here. What about history?"

"The Greenbrier Valley has a lot of history," Chelsea said, "and a few ghosts."

Erik glanced at Chelsea and smiled. I tried to think of something clever to say to get his eyes away from her, but I was speechless.

"We shouldn't forget the Potomac River. This river along with its Northern Branch form a border between West Virginia and Maryland," Brad said as he began to trace the North Branch of the Potomac.

"Wait, wait," Chelsea shouted as she waved both hands. "Big history here, the Fairfax Stone. It's in Tucker County. You know, Lord Fairfax and Charles II of England. Just trust me and mark that one."

"Okay, calm down little sister," Brad jokingly ordered. He looked over the map and began to make a list in the white areas of the legend. "Wheeling, Point Pleasant, Moundsville, Huntington, Charleston, New and Gauley Rivers, Greenbrier Valley, and the Fairfax Stone. These are definite. Anyplace else?"

"That's enough to start with," said Sakura as she pulled a small notebook from her purse and began to duplicate the list.

"Want to just split the list?" Brad asked.

9

"Don't forget the last part," I reminded them, "you know, *'attempt to find clues'* and *'knowledge is the key.'*"

"That's right," Chelsea agreed. "What kind of clues? Do you think more notes?"

"Or maybe," Morgan suggested, "the clues will come from *'strangers and friends?'*"

"I'm not sure about that," Brad responded. "We'll play it by ear. Let's see what kinds of clues we can find and go from there. We might need to change this list."

"I think we should do some searching in Charleston today," Sakura suggested.

"Me, too," said Morgan. "We could start with the capitol."

Ginny inquired as she pointed to the complex, "What about these other buildings?"

"Whoa," I pleaded. "I've been on a plane for almost six hours. Give me a break."

Erik's beautiful eyes turned to me as he apologized. "I'm sorry. We're not thinking very straight. Maybe we should meet back here later in the week?"

His soothing voice was interrupted as Chelsea remarked, "Oh, get over it, California. You'll be able to sleep your life away once we get to Welch."

"How about this?" Brad offered. "We'll spend two hours here. Sakura, Morgan, and Erik will start in the capitol. Chelsea, Ginny, we'll take the Cultural Center. We'll meet back here in exactly two hours. If we don't have anything, we'll . . . I'm not sure what we'll do. Just meet back here by four o'clock."

As heads nodded and all agreed, Brad began folding his map. Sakura, Morgan, and Erik slid off the bench as Chelsea and I moved away from the table. Our new friends walked down the ramp, off the steps and onto the walk. Just as they reached the giant magnolia trees bordering the walk leading to the west wing of the capitol, a horn sounded. Repeated honking caught everyone's attention as a small gray pickup truck sped down Greenbrier Street. An arm waved from the driver's window.

With a puzzled look on his face, Brad waved. He turned toward Chelsea and me and asked, "Any idea who that is?"

"Hey! That looks like the truck that tried to run me over at the airport," exclaimed Chelsea.

"Maybe he's coming back for a second chance," teased Brad.

10

"Ha! Ha!" Chelsea mimicked as the three of us moved toward the entrance of the Cultural Center.

FACTS

1. There are seven river drainage basins. All but one drain toward the west. The only eastern basin is the Potomac.

2. The western basins are the Monongahela, Little Kanawha, Kanawha, New, Guyandotte, Big Sandy, and Ohio.

3. Rivers of West Virginia:

Big Sandy	Birch
Blackwater	Cacapon
Cheat	Cherry
Coal	Cranberry
Elk	Gauley
Greenbrier	Guyandotte
Hughes	Kanawha
Little Coal	Little Kanawha
Lost	Monongahela
Mud	New
North Branch Potomac	Ohio
Pocatalico	Potomac
Shenandoah	South Branch Potomac
Stony	Tug
Tygart	West Fork
Williams	

4. Dolly Sods, in Tucker County, is a barren heath. It is home to glacial plant life and many woodland creatures. The snowshoe hare, bobcats, hawks and flying squirrels live freely across 10,000 acres of humus soil. This area was used as an artillery practice range during World War II.

5. Cranberry Glades, in Pocahontas County, is 750 acres of spongy bogs. It is home to rare glacial plants found usually on the tundra. Arctic flora, including reindeer moss, the carnivorous sundew and snake-in-the-mouth orchid can be found throughout this 55-square-mile area.

6. The Vandalia Gathering began in 1976 in Charleston. This is a traditional mountain music competition complete with dancing and crafts. It also hosts a Liar's Contest in which participants compete for the Golden Shovel Award.

Chapter 2

Clue from a Ghost

I felt so confused when I entered the Cultural Center for the second time. What should I look for, a stranger, a note, a horseshoe? I followed Brad and Chelsea as they moved quickly to the left and down the ramp. The quilts and display cases seemed a blur as I rounded the corner and almost ran head first into the Conestoga wagon.

"Here's the plan," Brad directed. "Chelsea, you go right and check out the exhibits on the Paleo Indians and the Woodland Indians. If nothing turns up there, go toward the back to the section on industry. Look over the glass-blowing and marble displays. Ginny, you take the Civil War in West Virginia exhibition and the two rooms on World Wars I and II. Oh, and be sure to look through this Conestoga wagon."

"Oh, I guess you're going to go to lunch while we work," scoffed Chelsea.

"No, little sister," Brad answered. "I'll search the log cabin, the general store, all the old telephones, plus the room on steamboats and the flatboat. If that meets with your approval?"

"Okay, okay," muttered Chelsea.

"Just what do we look for?" I asked.

"I'm not really sure. Just look for anything that might be related to a horseshoe," Brad replied.

"And if we find something...?" Chelsea inquired.

"Come for the other two," said Brad. "Let's go. We only have two hours."

"Good luck," I called as my cousins left in opposite directions to begin the search.

I cautiously moved toward the Conestoga wagon. The plaque on the side of the wagon described it as nine feet wide and nineteen feet long.

Most of these wagons, built in Lancaster, Pennsylvania, had blue bodies with red running gears and white canvas tops. They were ideal for carrying heavy loads across steep mountains because of their large wheels and sturdy brakes. It took six horses to pull one. Horses! Horseshoes! I peered around the end of the wagon and looked around the room. No security guards anywhere. I placed my backpack on the floor near the front wheel, put my hands on the rough wooden boards, stepped one foot on the axle, and pulled myself over the side and into the wagon. I was standing in between several burlap bags labeled "flour," "sugar," and "meal." They reminded me of the thirty-pound bags of mulch Mom would buy to put in her flower garden. I lifted each of the bags, but none was open. I saw two small kegs and a wooden chest. One keg had nails and the other had coal. I opened the wooden chest. It was like the one Chelsea and I found in the coal bin at Grandma's. It had a Bible, hornbook, crockery, and bed linens. No sign of a horseshoe. Nothing.

"Hey! You! Get down from there," shouted the young man who had been sitting at the reception desk. "No one is allowed in the wagon."

"Oh, I'm so sorry," I replied as I jumped to the floor. "I didn't see a sign. . . ."

He glared at me and said, "There are a few things we just expect people to know. If I see you in there again, or touching any open displays, I'll have to ask you to leave. Do you understand me, young lady?"

"Yes sir," I replied. "I was just leaving this room. I'm really sorry."

I grabbed my backpack and scurried left toward the military rooms. My heart was beating wildly. I knew I wasn't in any real trouble, but I didn't like people yelling at me. I walked slowly by World War I uniforms, weapons, a Red Cross flag, and gas masks. I was eager to make my way into the Civil War area when I noticed a glass-encased replica of the battleship, *USS WEST VIRGINIA*. Two magnificent bells, one hanging and one sitting near the replica, were inscribed *USS WEST VIRGINIA* 1922.

I had heard about this battleship. It was sunk at Pearl Harbor. I decided the horseshoe would just have to wait a bit, and I started to read the ship's history. One hundred five men were killed aboard this ship on December 7, 1941, when the Japanese bombed the naval base in Hawaii. The ship was repaired and returned to duty July 4, 1944. It was nicknamed the "Ghost of Pearl" as it plied the waters of the Pacific theater wrecking havoc on the Japanese. It received five battle stars.

"Mommy! Mommy! See big bell," exclaimed a small redheaded

toddler as he pointed toward the bell suspended in the wooden frame. He proceeded to lie on the floor to look upward into the bell. He crawled upon one knee and tried to reach the clapper. He rose to both knees and reached with tiny outstretched hands, "Ring, please," he pleaded, looking toward his Mother.

"No, No, you mustn't touch, Billy," his mother said gently.

The little boy reached up and pulled down a piece of paper. He handed it to his Mother and again asked, "Ring, please,"

"What have you done," the woman muttered to herself as she looked at the paper.

"What in the world is this?" As she read the note, with a puzzled look on her face, she turned and noticed I was watching her. Looking in my direction she asked, "Did you lose something, a note maybe?"

"What does it say?" I inquired eagerly.

"It really doesn't make sense," she offered. "It says, *'A pearl is a treasure, but not the one you seek. Travel around the river bends and into the mountains deep.'*"

"That is mine," I gasped. "It's a clue. . . ." I didn't know how to explain.

"Are you on a scavenger hunt?" the woman asked with a smile on her face.

"Yeah, sort of," I answered.

"Here is your note," she remarked handing me the slip of paper. "Come on Billy, we've had enough for one day." She turned and took Billy's hand and started toward the exit.

"Thank you," I called after her as she started up the ramp.

"You're welcome," replied Billy, looking over his shoulder and squeezing his Mother's hand. His little legs seemed to dance as he tried to keep up with his mother.

"Travel around river bends and into mountains deep" I thought as I hurried around the corner and passed the telephone switchboard. "Brad, Brad," I called. His head appeared around the side of the raft and I continued. "You won't believe it. I've got a clue."

"You're kidding," Brad exclaimed as he jumped over the side of the raft. "I really didn't expect to find anything today," he sputtered as he reached for the slip of paper.

"In the World War II room," I began to explain "I was just reading about the *USS WEST VIRGINIA*, and this little kid was on the floor under the ship's bell. He pulled this piece of paper down and handed it to his

15

Mother. She read it. . . ."

"*'Travel around river bends and into mountains deep,'*" where could that be?" questioned Brad as he looked toward the ceiling. "You know, we may need to add another place to the list, one deep inside a mountain with a river nearby. You think it could be the exhibition coal mine in Beckley?"

"Beats me," I responded. "I don't have a clue. Maybe Chelsea. . . ."

"Sure, just leave me wandering in the marbles," said Chelsea with a faked hurt look on her face. "I am a part of this, too, you know."

"I was coming to get you," I explained. "I just happened to be closer to Brad."

"Yeah, sure," she groaned.

"Knock it off, little sis. We don't have time for you to pout. Put your brain to work on this clue: *'A pearl is a treasure, but not the one you seek. Travel around the river bends and into the mountains deep.'* Any ideas?" Brad asked.

"*Travel around the river bends,*" Chelsea muttered. "*Mountains deep.*" Well, how about the coalmine in Beckley? Any river there? The New River Gorge. It's cut really deep and it created the mountains. *'River bends'* Hey! Lost River in Hardy County! The River begins near Brock's Gap and disappears into the earth under Sandy Ridge. It travels about two miles underground and reappears as the source of the Cacapon River. Now that's around a river bend and it goes into a mountain deep."

I looked at Chelsea in amazement and remarked, "You sound like an encyclopedia. How do you know all this stuff?"

"West Virginia History," she answered with a bit of pride in her voice, "It's required. I had a really good teacher, too. That always helps."

"We still have about twenty minutes left. Let's see if we can find Sakura and the others," suggested Brad.

Chelsea and I followed Brad as he started up the ramp and through the lobby. He kept looking at the note as we followed him across the lawn and into the west wing.

"They could be anywhere in the capitol," I said.

"Don't forget; strangers and friends can help," Chelsea reminded me.

"You're right. A stranger gave me that clue. I would have never looked inside a bell. This is weird," I replied as a shiver ran up my spine.

Brad opened the door for Chelsea and me to enter. The minute I stepped inside, I noticed the beautiful painted ceiling. The panels showed

16

women carrying leafy branches and sheaves of wheat.

"This is really neat," I gushed as I surveyed the ceiling. "Is this real marble on these walls?"

"Yes, it is," Chelsea answered, "the east and west wings were constructed first. The architect designed these elaborate ceilings; but the main building was constructed during a depression, so it is not so fancy. Those ceilings and walls are not decorated."

We walked down the corridor toward the Governor's reception room. The door was open and I noticed a blue oriental carpet and a beautiful chandelier suspended over a long table. Two desks were located on opposite sides of the entry way and several people were milling about.

"No sign of them," commented Brad. "Let's head for the rotunda."

We turned left and I realized what Chelsea was telling me earlier. The ceilings were plain and only pictures of past governors dotted the walls. Up ahead I saw Sakura and Morgan, with heads tilted back, looking upward. Erik was lying on the floor.

Brad shouted, "What happened?"

We began to run down the corridor toward the trio. Erik raised his head as Morgan and Sakura turned.

"Oh, Erik just wanted a better look at the chandelier. He insisted the view from the floor was the best," Sakura explained.

"Take a look for yourself," Erik insisted. "I think there is something up there. We've looked everywhere else. If I were going to stash the horseshoe, I'd put it in that chandelier."

Chelsea offered, "That would make sense. It would be safe there, and it would still be on state property."

"How do you go about searching for it?" scoffed Morgan. "We've already asked, and the security guard said the chandelier is only lowered every four years. So the horseshoe can't be up there."

"Why every four years?" I asked.

"Because they clean it before each governor's inauguration. It takes three and one-half hours to lower it, two days to clean it, and four and one-half hours to raise it back into place," answered Morgan. "It's not an easy job."

"Then the last time it was lowered was last January," Brad calculated.

"Right," remarked Sakura, "so it's not up there. We've got nothing to add to the search."

"We've had better luck," said Brad. "Ginny was given this note in the Cultural Center." He handed the note to Sakura as Erik and Morgan rushed to peer over her shoulder.

"Pearls . . . but I thought the horseshoe had diamonds and sapphires?" Sakura said.

"Pearl was referring to Pearl Harbor. I found the note in the World War II exhibit near the battleship replica of the *USS WEST VIRGINIA*. A stranger, well really her son, found it inside the ship's bell."

"The ship was sunk during the attack on Pearl Harbor, but was put back into service in the Pacific. It was nicknamed the 'Ghost of Pearl' because it destroyed so many enemy ships without being found," Chelsea lectured.

With a perplexed look on her face, Sakura asked, "Where do we look for a river bend and mountains deep?"

"Today, nowhere," said Brad. "We have to get Ginny to Grandma's. Then we'll make a decision as to where to start."

"Thank you!" I replied. "I'm beat. Besides, my head is swimming with all of this missing treasure, mountain lore, and knowledge stuff."

"Hey! California girl, they're offering a reward. Don't wimp out on us now," commented Chelsea.

"Give her a break," said Brad. "We need some time to think about this anyway. There's no need to run around in circles."

"I agree," Sakura replied. "I need to talk with Miss Becky before I obligate Morgan and Erik. She may not want us to help."

Erik interrupted, "Are you kidding? She'd love something like this. She may even have some ideas as to where to look."

"I hope so," Morgan offered.

"Let's exchange phone numbers and e-mail addresses," Brad said to Sakura. "We'll keep in touch."

Sakura began writing her phone number and e-mail address on the back of a Cultural Center brochure and handed it to Brad. She smiled warmly at him as he took the card.

"I'll be in touch," promised Brad looking into her eyes.

"Hey, big brother," Chelsea said breaking the spell, "we all have e-mail addresses."

The four of us exchanged addresses and said our good-byes. We agreed to rethink the clues and study the map before making any other decisions or excursions.

We walked our new friends to Sakura's white Jeep. As they climbed inside, I noticed Sakura's vanity tag, 'Nugget.'

18

"Chelsea," I whispered as I nudged her arm. "get a load of that license plate."

"Nugget, like the Golden Horseshoe is a nugget of gold," murmured Chelsea.

I felt another strange summer coming on as I watched the white Jeep turn down Virginia Street. I had to admit that my summers in West Virginia were anything but dull.

Brad turned and clapped his hands. "Let's head for home," he suggested. We fell in step behind him as he headed toward his white Camry.

"I'll take the back seat," I offered. "I just want to sleep."

"That's fine with me," agreed Chelsea. "You just snooze away until we get to Welch. It'll take about four hours."

I tossed my backpack onto the seat and bundled an old sweater around it. This would serve as my pillow for the next few hours. Brad put in a CD and Chelsea snuggled down in her seat. I curled my legs onto the seat and closed my eyes. I felt the car lurch as we left the parking lot and turned right to reach I-64. The sounds of the engine and the CD seemed to complement each other, as the car moved ever so gently down the road. I tried to push thoughts about the missing horseshoe out of my mind. I concentrated on seeing my grandmother, the house where my mom grew up, and my Uncle Ron and Aunt Fran. It would be nice to visit Franklin's Dairy and get one of those great chocolate shakes. My eyes were getting heavy, and my thoughts seemed fuzzy as I drifted asleep.

Brad slammed on the breaks, throwing me onto the floor. A siren wailed. Chelsea was saying something to Brad as she leaned out the car window. I pulled myself up and strained my eyes to see what lay ahead. A huge semi was pulled to the side of the road and a police car's blue lights were flashing. The siren became a faint wail as I tried to focus my eyes. It was dusk, and fog was beginning to roll in over the mountain peaks. We seemed to be in an abyss that was surrounded by lush green mountains.

"Where are we?" I asked.

"Bender's Bridge," replied Brad. "I'm not sure if this semi was caught speeding or if he was run off the road."

"Look! Look up there," Chelsea shouted, "on the other side of the bridge. That's the gray truck we saw at the airport. You know, the one that nearly took me out."

"So what?" replied Brad. "He has a right to be on this road."

"It just seems strange to me that it shows up all the time," Chelsea said.

Brad moved slowly past the semi and the police car. He crossed the bridge and began a slow climb up the next mountain.

I snuggled back into my makeshift bed and tucked my hands under my face. "Let me know when we reach Grandma's, okay?" I said.

Chelsea answered, "Will do."

The next thing I felt was Chelsea gently shaking my shoulders. "We're here. Grandma is standing on the porch," she whispered.

I blinked and tried to clear my head. *Here* must mean Welch. It must be Grandma's because a beacon was shining into the car. Grandma calls it a front porch light, but it's bright enough to light up three blocks. I rose on one arm and silently told my legs to move. With my other arm, I reached for my backpack and turned to see my grandma in a gray flannel robe standing on her clay-tiled front porch. I waved and moved my aching body out of the car.

Brad was pulling my luggage out of the trunk when he said, "See, Grandma, safe and sound. Now you have two granddaughters this summer, and I will have peace and quiet at home."

Shuffling down the steps, Grandma embraced me as soon as I climbed out of the car. "Oh, Ginny," she wept, "it's so good to have you back. I made some blueberry muffins just for you and Chelsea. Now come on in and have a bite before you go to bed."

"For Ginny and Chelsea, Grandma, how could you?" Brad teased. "I'd be offended if I didn't know that you really liked me best."

Grandma replied with a twinkle in her eye, "Hush now, I want none of that bickering this summer." She put her arm around my shoulder as the two of us started up the steps. "I've made up the room downstairs for you and Chelsea, but I left the computer upstairs on the desk in the hallway. We'll have to share it, " she added.

"Oh, Ginny," Chelsea began, "I forgot to tell you that Grandma is 'high tech' now. She surfs the net, sends e-mail, and loves to shop online. But she has this hang-up about 'Free Cell.' She is addicted to the game."

"That's okay, Grandma," I stated. "I feel the same way about 'Solitaire.'"

Grandma maneuvered us toward the kitchen as Brad struggled with the luggage. This was my favorite place in her house. It always smelled good and looked bright with the white cabinets, white furniture, and yellow ruffled curtains. A long back porch, with a view of a small creek and a looming mountain, seemed to shield the house from any danger. As Grandma set a tray of her famous muffins on the table, Chelsea got glasses from the cupboard and milk from the refrigerator. Grandma listened attentively as I told her the latest about Mom, Dad, and David. Chelsea chimed in as I told about my flight, our new friends, and the search at the Capitol Complex.

Coming into the kitchen, Brad commented, "This looks like an old hens' party to me. I'd better get out of here." He picked up two muffins in one hand and waved with the other. "I'll see you girls in the morning."

"Thanks, Brad," I said.

"Yes, dear," said Grandma, "thank you for getting my girls here. Take some muffins for your mom and dad. I'll have Chelsea call you when she gets up tomorrow."

Brad stacked two more muffins on his folded arm and headed for the door.

Placing her palms on the table, Grandma pushed herself into a standing position. "These old bones need to get to bed. Now, you young people can sit up all night or go to bed any time you feel like it. I'll see you in the morning." She gave each of us a kiss on the forehead.

"Night, Grandma," said Chelsea.

"Good night, Grandma," I echoed. Turning to Chelsea I continued, "I'm beat. Let's put the glasses in the sink and head on to bed."

"I'm with you. Let's go," she responded.

We put the remaining muffins in the breadbox and set the glasses in the sink. Chelsea remembered to put water in the glasses since grandma didn't have a dishwasher. I suddenly recalled the one and only reason I didn't like visiting my grandma, washing dishes. Everything else was great. Chelsea and I talked very little as we prepared for bed. We both agreed it had been a long day. I don't even remember saying good night, just my head hitting the pillow.

The first few days in Welch seemed normal enough. Chelsea and I went swimming every day at Linkups Park Pool. Brad would meet up with us occasionally and as always we discussed "around the river bends and in the mountains deep." We weren't the only ones trying to decipher this message. Morgan, Erik, and Sakura e-mailed us daily with ideas as to where to look. Chelsea called her West Virginia history teacher, Mrs. Klinestiver, and asked for help. Finally, we came to a conclusion.

"Morgan, Erik, Mrs. Klinestiver, Chelsea, and I all agree. It's got to be on the New River," I insisted. "That's five to two. Majority rules. Let's check it out."

"I know this sounds a little far-fetched, but hear me out. Sakura and I think it is a possibility that *"in the mountains deep"* could mean the inner workings, the idea for a separate state," Brad argued. "I think Wheeling, where the state was born, might be a good place to look. You have a river, physical mountains, and you could argue the state had deep psychological mountains to overcome before statehood. That all happened in Wheeling. We think the missing horseshoe has to be there."

"But deep," interrupted Chelsea, "could refer to the time it took to cut through the mountains. The New River is at least 65 million years old. That's 'deep' enough for me."

"It has lots of bends," I added.

"Hey, you don't have to keep hammering on the New River. Sakura and I would enjoy a rafting trip, alone," Brad said.

"Not so fast. I'm ahead of you on this one. Mom and Grandma said it would be okay if Ginny and I go. We're old enough to whitewater raft on the New River. Minimum age is fourteen," argued Chelsea.

"Great," I exclaimed. "When did you ask?" I knew if Aunt Fran would allow Chelsea to go, my Mom would also approve.

Chelsea replied, "After I heard from Erik that they could go, I asked Mom. Remember e-mail, bro. I can always keep in touch."

Chelsea was e-mailing Erik, too. I wonder if she knows I have also been writing Erik. He never said a word about whitewater rafting or corresponding with Chelsea.

"Hey, it's all right," commented Brad in an adult tone. "As long as Sakura is along I'll take you kids wherever you need to go. When do you children want to go?"

"Knock it off," Chelsea ordered. "We're not babies."

I suggested, "Brad, why don't you check with Sakura and see if they can go on Thursday?"

"I'm on my way," Brad replied as he went down the hall toward the computer.

I looked at my cousin and wondered what was going on between Erik and her. Maybe I should just forget about him. Chelsea always seemed to get the great guys. I couldn't resist asking, "Do you e-mail Erik a lot?"

"Never," Chelsea answered. "I was on line one day and got an IM from him. He said they really wanted to go rafting and asked if I could help at this end. So once I talked Mom into it, she called your mother, and we were on our way. Old Cherry Blossom. . . ."

"Cherry Blossom," I giggled, "who are you talking about?"

"Sakura," replied Chelsea. "Her name translated means Cherry

Blossom. Erik thinks she has a thing for Brad. She has been working Miss Becky really hard to let them go. So I knew it would only be a matter of time before Brad would get off this Wheeling kick."

"No kidding," I scoffed as I wondered again if Erik had a thing for Chelsea. He had been e-mailing me a couple of times a day, and I enjoyed chatting with him.

Brad announced as he walked into the room, "Sakura said Thursday isn't a good day for her. Miss Becky has car problems and is using Sakura's jeep. I offered. . ."

"Maybe we should call her Crab Apple instead of Cherry Blossom," teased Chelsea.

"How did you know, Chelsea? Have you been reading my e-mail?" an angry Brad asked.

"No," announced Chelsea, "but I do know how to use a Japanese-American dictionary."

"What about Friday?" I asked.

"We can still make it Thursday if you girls don't mind an extra hour of driving each way," remarked Brad.

"Why would we do that?" Chelsea asked.

"So I could pick them up in Belle. Then the six of us would travel the old Midland Trail to Hawks Nest and Hico. We'll whitewater out of Hico with the North American River Rafters. They have a good safety record," Brad explained.

Sounds good to me," I said.

"No problem," Chelsea agreed.

When Brad left the room to call Sakura, Chelsea gave me a high five and shouted, "This is great! Whitewater rafting!"

FACTS

1. West Virginia's first capitol, (1863-1870), was located in Wheeling. The second capitol, (1870-1875), was erected in Charleston at a cost of $79,000. The third capitol, 1875-1885, was rebuilt in Wheeling. The fourth capitol, (1885-1921), was built in Charleston, but it burned January 3, 1921.

2. Cass Gilbert of Zanesville, Ohio, designed West Virginia's fifth capitol. His other works include the world's first skyscraper, the state capitols of Minnesota and Arkansas, the U.S. Treasury Building, and the U. S. Supreme Court Building.

3. The present Capitol in Charleston took eight years to complete at a cost of ten million dollars.

4. It was constructed in three phases. The west wing was built in 1924-1925, the east wing was constructed in 1926-27, and the rotunda connecting the wings was completed in 1930-32.

5. A 4,000-pound chandelier, made of 10,000 pieces of Czechoslovakian crystal, hangs on a 54-foot, gold-plated chain, 180 feet from the floor in the columned rotunda. This chandelier is eight feet in diameter and is illuminated by 96 light bulbs.

6. The chandelier is cleaned every four years prior to the governor's inauguration. It takes three and one-half hours to lower it, two days to clean each of its 10,000 pieces of cut crystal, and four and one-half hours to raise the chandelier back into place.

7. The Supreme Court chambers, located on the third floor of the east wing, was the model for the U.S. Supreme Court.

8. The *USS West Virginia* commissioned December 1, 1923, at the Norfolk Navy Yard sustained severe damage during the Japanese attack on Pearl Harbor, December 7, 1941. One hundred five men died as the vessel sank upright. The 31,888-ton battleship was raised on May 7, 1942, and returned to fleet duty on July 4, 1944.

9. This battleship, referred to as the "Ghost of Pearl," earned five battle stars. Her personnel received 28 awards and ten letters of commendation for outstanding service.

10. The Beckley Exhibition Coal Mine in Raleigh County is an authentic example of coal mining when a pick and shovel were the norm. Visitors go through 1,500 feet of dark tunnels riding in a man-trip mine trolley.

Chapter 3

Around the River Bend

On Thursday Chelsea and I got up before Grandma called us. We splashed on sunscreen and pulled on bathing suits before dressing in shorts and tee shirts. We put baseball caps, sunglasses, and extra sunscreen in my backpack. Chelsea gave me an old pair of her tennis shoes to wear, since Mom always sent me with new white ones.We reached the kitchen just as Brad pulled into the driveway.

"He's here. Sorry Grandma, but we don't have time to eat," I said.

"I figured as much so I packed you a little snack," she said smiling.

"You're an angel," said Chelsea as she looked inside the paper bag. "Pop tarts, strawberry, frosted ones. They're my favorite."

"I put in some brown sugar cinnamon for you, Ginny," Grandma said as she patted my arm. "There is orange juice in the black thermos and milk in the red one. Now you girls, and you, young man, be very careful."

Giving her a hug and a kiss, I said, "Thanks Grandma. You're the best."

"Don't worry. I will be," said Brad reaching for some bananas in the fruit bowl. "Mind if I take a few of these?"

"Help yourself," Grandma offered. "Take a few apples, too."

Brad dropped three apples and three bananas in the bag with the pop tarts. Chelsea folded the top of the bag and gave Grandma a kiss. Brad grabbed the black thermos and I picked up the red one. I was so excited about rafting and seeing Erik that I felt myself almost running out the front door. We waved at Grandma as Brad pulled out of the driveway.

It was too early to eat and too dark to see much along the highway, so Chelsea and I decided to sleep on the way to Belle. Brad had borrowed Uncle Ron's van so we had plenty of room to stretch out. Chelsea had climbed into the long third seat, put on her disc player earphones and never said another word. I reclined in the captain's seat behind the driver in the second row and pulled an old afghan over me. Brad had the radio on and was singing softly. I gazed for a while out the window watching shapes and blurs pass by. The warmth of the afghan and pleasant thoughts of the hours ahead soon put me to sleep.

"Hey! Hey! It's so good to know you're excited to see us," said a voice that sounded familiar. "We've been waiting for you to get here."

Sun was shining in my face and van doors were being opened. Morgan was standing next to my seat but moving toward the back seat to sit with Chelsea.

Erik stepped inside carrying a large McDonald's bag and said, "Good morning, ladies. Mind if we join you? I've got breakfast, Egg McMuffins all around."

"Erik," I gasped, "I. . . . We are excited to see all of you. Grandma packed us some snacks, but yours smell better. What time is it anyway?"

"We'll eat hers later," said Chelsea from the back.

"It's six thirty, or near that," Erik replied as he passed out the McMuffins and cartons of milk. The four of us unwrapped the food and began to eat and talk at the same time. Morgan and Erik chatted about their activities the last few days and agreed with us that today's trip was going to be awesome. Brad and Sakura stood outside the van and talked. After five minutes into their conversation, Chelsea decided it was time to give her big brother a nudge.

"Hey, big bro, let's go," she shouted.

Walking around to the passenger's side, Brad opened the door for Sakura. "Please be patient," he said to Sakura. "We must prove there isn't a golden horseshoe in or near the New River. Instead, we will need to make a trip to Wheeling."

"Yeah, whatever," replied Chelsea, rolling her eyes.

Brad climbed into the driver's seat and pulled onto Route 60, traveling east. Every few miles I would see a sign referring to this route as the Midland Trail. The valley floor made a winding path through lush green mountains. Summer in California was brown and dry, but here everything looked deep green and cool. At intervals, small villages would appear, with a few houses, a church, a service station, and some local eateries. Produce stands, selling homegrown vegetables, dotted both sides of the roadway. And what a road it was. There were only two lanes, divided by yellow lines drawn length wise down the center. Brad explained later that those lines meant drivers were not to pass other cars. As we crawled around blind curves and dropped over hills without knowing what would come next, I was reminded of video games I had played. For miles, the river, the railroad tracks, and the Midland Trail filled the valley floor causing houses and churches to perch on the mountainside. I noticed a sign on the right-hand side of the trail identifying the London Locks and Dam and one on the left stating "Cannelton Industries."

"Cannelton Industries," said Chelsea, "I had that in school. Not the industries, but cannel coal. It's a special kind of coal that has a lot of oil in it. In fact, people in Kanawha County used it for lighting purposes as early as the late 1700s."

"Chelsea," warned Brad, "you're beginning to sound like Mom."

My Aunt Fran was a teacher. She loved to share trivia, which she thought was valuable, with anyone in hearing distance. Aunt Fran would start practically every sentence with, "Did you know. . . ." Then a history lesson would follow.

"It's true. It was also used in the production of salt," added Chelsea. "I was just trying to make the drive interesting."

"What can you tell me about this place, Alloy?" asked Erik pointing to a sign.

Getting excited about contributing information, Chelsea gushed, "The Kanawha Valley is loaded with minerals. That's why all of the chemical plants are in and around Charleston. The earliest mineral extracted from the river was brine salt. Have you ever heard of Booker T. Washington, the famous black educator? His mother's husband worked as a slave for the Ruffners in the salt industries."

"Salt, salt," said a puzzled Morgan. "I thought West Virginia was all about coal."

"Coal was mined later," Chelsea continued. "Salt was the first major industry in West Virginia."

"What a view," Sakura remarked at the sight of two sets of falls across an extremely wide expanse of the Kanawha River. "Is that a bed and breakfast?" she asked pointing to a large two-story dwelling built of hand-made bricks.

"Pull over, Brad," pleaded Chelsea. "This place is really neat. It has a lot of history."

"We have time, don't we?" asked Sakura, putting her hand on Brad's arm.

He turned right so quickly I slid off my captain's chair. Erik reached out to catch me and I forgot all about the falls, salt, and even rafting. He opened the door and held my hand as I climbed down from the van. Brad helped Sakura down as Chelsea and Morgan scrambled out.

"Glen Ferris Inn, 1839," read Brad. "Now that's old, even before the Civil War."

"Check out this marker," Erik remarked as he read, "'Located from this point across the Kanawha River, was a Civil War camp for the Union Army, 1862-64. The site had 56 cabins and parade grounds for the 23rd Ohio Volunteer Infantry, commanded by Col. Rutherford B. Hayes and Lt. William McKinley, future United States presidents.'"

"This is really a neat town," I commented as I turned full circle to take in the falls, a park, and the houses on the left of the road. American flags were displayed on each telephone pole and the lawn in front of each brick home was immaculate. Brightly colored flowers bordered walkways in the sparkling clear sunshine.

"I don't want to be the bad guy, but we need to get going," said Brad. We've got to be in Hico by eight thirty."

I shouted, "Then let's go."

I led the way, climbing into the van and everyone settled into his or her original seats. Brad pulled onto the road, and the van started to climb upward as the mountain became steeper. We clawed our way up and down narrow passages and coiled around hairpin curves. A steady flow of huge trucks, heaped with logs, rumbled past us toward Charleston. A log cabin, bearing the sign Appalachian Arts and Crafts, sat in the middle of the road. The van swerved left and continued upward. A sign advertising a snake pit, and an old Volkswagen driven into the side of a building, came into view. Painted on the side of the building were the words "Mystery Hole."

"We have nothing like this in California, not even Venus Beach," I said in amazement.

"It gets better," Erik replied. "Just wait 'til you see Hawks Nest."

"Is it anything like the snake pit?" I asked seriously.

Erik chuckled and answered, "No, it's a state park and they have a beautiful lodge. There, there it is," he continued as he pointed to a modern lodge sitting high atop a hill. "Are we going to stop?"

"Maybe on the trip back," said Brad. "We're almost to Hico. Another fifteen minutes and we'll be there."

I read signs pointing out the Canyon Rim Visitor Center, the New River Gorge, and advertisements for several rafting companies. Finally,

New River Gorge Bridge

a sign reading "North American River Rafters" came into view. Brad turned left and pulled into a graveled parking lot holding about fifteen cars. Three rustic frame buildings sprawled around an open area filled with wooden picnic tables and large, flat slabs of rock. A roofed bulletin board held the attention of would-be rafters as they checked schedules. A small building, marked for personnel only, sat on the right. Next to it stood a much larger building that served as a trading post and refreshment center. Situated on the far left was an equipment barn with its doors open, displaying bright yellow helmets, blue and red life vests, and aluminum oars with yellow plastic paddles. Kayaks were scattered throughout the compound, some only for decoration.

Brad announced, "We're here. Don't forget hats and sunscreen."

I clamored to grab my backpack, as Morgan and Chelsea came rushing out of the back seat before Erik could open the door. I felt like a squirrel as I scampered excitedly out of the van and followed Brad and Sakura into the trading post. I moved in line behind Morgan and Erik. The river guide explained the waiver that needed to be signed when the fee was paid.

"Sounds like he's saying if anything at all happens to you, it's your fault. So don't try to sue," I muttered to Chelsea.

"Welcome to adventure sports," Chelsea whispered.

The six of us signed in and paid. We were sent to the equipment barn to pick up blue life jackets, yellow helmets and oars. The red jackets were for the guides. We were then directed to take seats on an old school bus that had been repainted with the company's name and logo. The bus was almost filled when we boarded, but we found seats in the back. Brad, Sakura, and Morgan pushed their bodies into one seat. Like a champ, Brad just smiled and pulled Sakura closer toward him. A college-aged man moved across the aisle to sit with a buddy and offered his seat to Erik and me. Chelsea, without a second thought, sat with a perfect stranger and began a conversation.

Five guides entered, all wearing red vests. Three seats in the front of the bus were reserved for them. A middle-aged man handed several canvas bags and four coolers to the guides. He then climbed on and took a seat behind the steering wheel. As he turned the ignition, one of the guides stood up and braced his feet firmly on the floor between the two front seats.

"Yo, I need a heads up," he commanded. When the passengers quieted, he continued. "I'm Tim, leader for the day. Is there anyone on the bus who didn't sign the waiver or pay the fee? Good. Would everyone please hold the yellow pass you received over your head in your right hand." One of the other guides stood, counted the souls on board and nodded toward Tim.

Tim tapped the bus driver on the back and he released the brake. The old bus jostled us as it left the parking lot and chugged onto the main road. Dirt and gravel flew everywhere.

"Just relax and enjoy the ride," Tim said. "We will be on this highway for about five minutes and then onto a dirt road to reach the river. We'll put in at Cunard, raft for approximately two and one-half hours, have lunch, and continue down the New River and under the New River Gorge Bridge. This bus will pick us up at Teays Landing and bring us back to headquarters. Any questions?"

After a brief pause, Tim went on. "Let me introduce you to the other guides. Since ladies ought to go first, this is Hannah. Hard, hard, Hannah." He winked at the petite brunette when she stood and waved. "Next to Hannah is Coyote. If you hear him howling, it's best to ignore him." A sandy haired young man about Brad's age waved his hand without standing or turning around. "Over in this corner, is Grizzly, you know, like the bear." Grizzly stood, all six feet and three inches, and growled. He pawed at the air like a bear before he flopped his 250-pound body back into the seat. "On this side of the bus are the Professor and Mary-Anne. They escaped from the island and have been working for us for the last six years." The couple stood and waved to the crowd. "These two stay together like peanut butter and jelly."

The bus turned suddenly to the left and lunged over the mountainside. A few people screamed. Tim appeared calm as the bus swayed from side to side and tree limbs tried to push through the windows. I was pulled down into the seat and then rocketed up as the bus bounced across the terrain.

"This is the easy part," Tim joked. "We have a few miles left so I need you to listen up. Six of you will be in a rubber raft with one of these expert guides. Do exactly what the guide tells you to do, and do it when he tells you to. Is that clear? You must obey all directions. Your safety, as well as the safety of others, is at stake. There will be only three commands from your guide. The first is paddle." Tim held up an oar and demonstrated how to paddle. "The second is back paddle." He reversed the direction of the oar he was using. "The last is bail." He reached under the front seat and held a plastic bucket over his head. He demonstrated how to dip water and empty the bucket. Any questions?" Again he paused briefly. "Alrighttttt," he exaggerated, "we have a bright group. We'll be stopping soon. You will see five blue rafts along the riverbank, a guide in front of each. You may select any raft. If you want to be with friends, keep in mind only six passengers to a raft."

The bus came to an abrupt stop. Everyone fell forward as Tim grabbed the two rails on either side of the aisle. His body was stretched back and thrust forward.

"Safe," shouted Coyote jumping from his seat and imitating a baseball umpire.

"Let's give a hand to Blind Bat Bill for his driving skills," Tim shouted as laughter and applause moved from the back of the bus to the front.

Once the guides and equipment were off the bus, the rest of us followed in school-bus manner. Erik and I waited outside the bus for the rest of our group.

"Which one?" I asked looking at the rafts and people milling on the riverbank.

"The first three are already filled," Morgan remarked.

"How about Number 863?" Brad asked. "Coyote doesn't have anyone yet."

"Good idea," replied Erik.

We hurried toward Coyote. He looked in our direction and waved two other rafters off. "I think that's my six," he said nodding toward us. When we reached the raft, he held up his hand. "Put the life jackets and helmets on now. Helmets over ball caps give you extra protection. Toss anything you might be holding into the raft. Three of you on each side, as we pull this baby into the water."

I was sure glad I was wearing Chelsea's old tennis shoes. Sakura, Eric, and Morgan got on one side, Brad, Chelsea, and I on the other. We waded into the cold, crystal water and took hold of the handgrips on the side of the raft. I felt something brush against my lower leg. I stopped myself from screaming and shook my leg. How soon before I get into the boat, I wondered. Water was barely above my knees when I heard Coyote give another howl. This time, I did jump.

"That means get in," said Coyote as we struggled to climb into the raft.

Brad and Sakura moved to the front rubber bench. Erik and I took the second row, and I immediately positioned my left foot into a canvas foot harness. I was beginning to have second thoughts about this trip. Chelsea and Morgan wanted the back seat so they could be close to Coyote. He took his seat on the far end of the raft and proceeded to stow a canvas bag and cooler on opposite sides of his feet. He tied both objects securely to foot harnesses on the floor of the raft.

"Practice time," announced Coyote as he held an oar for us to see. "Hold the oar firmly, with both hands. Keep an eye on the person in front of you. You want to dip your oar in the water at the same time, pull back, and lift the oar out of the water. All together now, dip, pull, lift, dip, pull, lift — one more time — dip, pull and lift. Now let's do some back paddling. The only difference is you dip behind you, push the bottom of the oar forward and lift. Together now, dip behind, push forward and lift, dip behind, push forward, and lift. Way to go, guys. I've got winners. You see three plastic buckets, one for each row of seats. Is there anyone here who doesn't know how to bail?" This brought laughter from the group.

While swaying gently in the raft, I smelled rich soil and pine needles drifting around me. The sounds of the other rafters laughing and the splashing of oars floated through the morning air. The sun pushed its way through the dew-laden trees and warmed my body. I was brought back to reality when an oar nudged my foot.

Erik, with a big smile on his face asked, "Having fun?"

"Certainly," I responded.

"Now for the most important thing of all. If you should come out of the raft DON'T PANIC. Sit into the river, keep your feet up, and face forward." Coyote demonstrated this position when he jumped into the river. He instructed, "Feet up, I don't want any heads banged against the rocks. The forest rangers in these parts hate blood getting into their rivers." He continued as he climbed back in the raft, "Besides, I don't want to ruin my reputation. I am allotted two drownings a year, and my quota is filled."

All rafters practiced rowing and back rowing for about five minutes. I noticed other guides jumping in and out of rafts amid peels of laughter. Finally, Tim blew a whistle and pointed his oar toward Coyote. Coyote nodded.

"We're lead, guys," he said. "So do me proud. Row!"

We began to row toward the center of the river. Once in the center, Coyote had us stop rowing and the current carried us gently forward. I heard another whistle and Grizzly's raft put in. Whistles were repeated until Tim in the final raft was on the water. Our raft was moving faster now, and I could hear the roar and see the foam of whitewater up ahead.

Coyote shouted, "Heads up. We're about to go through Pinball Rapid. When I say row, start to row."

The raft moved faster and my heart raced. The front of the raft dipped downward and water splashed over Brad and Sakura. It covered the entire floor of the raft.

"ROW, ROW," commanded Coyote.

I tried to concentrate on dipping, pulling, and lifting. The raft swerved to the left, dipped, and water splashed over Erik and Morgan. I think I was still rowing when the raft lunged to the right, and this time Chelsea and I were soaked. All of a sudden the raft slowed down and we began to glide in a pool of water.

"Left side only, row," Coyote said in a normal voice. "Let's see how the others do."

Our raft turned sideways and gently bobbed. We bailed water from the floor of the raft as we watched the others come through the rapid. Once Tim's raft was through, everyone clapped and yelled.

"You guys did great. Now we have two Class IV rapids coming up. We may be on the river, but we'll be riding the Upper Railroad and the Lower Railroad," announced Coyote.

We continued down the New River through endless rapids called Lost

Lunch, Ender Waves, Piece of Cake, and Hip Kick. It felt like being on a roller coaster as we rose and fell in the crashing waves. We put in on the riverbank near huge flat rocks and helped the guides unpack food and drinks for lunch. We spread our wet t-shirts and shorts on the flat rocks to dry as we, in our bathing suits, soaked up the warm rays of the sun.

Tim blew his whistle. Just like an army, everyone rose, dressed, and headed toward the guides and rafts. Life jackets and helmets were hurriedly put into place so the rafts could be pulled into the water. As before, each raft put in as signaled by the whistle. We ran three Class IV rapids in a row, The Keeneys, The Greyhound, and the Double Z. We slowed to Class II rapids with the Upper and Lower Kaymoors, Miller's Folly and Thread the Needle. Next we floated under the New River Gorge Bridge and enjoyed body surfing in the gentle water. Before long, we reached Fayette Station. With sunburned faces, aching arms, and victorious weariness, we pulled the rafts onto the bank. Blind as a Bat Bill was waiting with the school bus.

"This is the best day I've ever had," exclaimed Chelsea.

Morgan agreed, "Same here."

Erik remarked, "It was great, wasn't it?"

"Oh, yes," I replied, "I've never done anything like this before. But I didn't find any clues about the missing horseshoe."

"I totally forgot the horseshoe," Chelsea gasped.

Morgan asked Erik, "Did you see anything?"

Brad interrupted, "No, because it isn't here. I'm telling you, we need to go to Wheeling."

Sakura said, "He's right, you know."

"What a surprise," Chelsea whispered to Morgan. "She agrees with Brad."

Morgan grinned and nudged Brad with her elbow.

We boarded the bus and fell exhausted into our seats. Erik offered his shoulder as a pillow, and soon I was sound asleep. The bus coming to a sudden stop jerked me awake. No one stood this time. Exhausted, we patiently waited in our seats to disembark. As we ambled toward the parking lot, a gray truck sped off the lot and onto the highway. A horn blew and the driver waved.

Chelsea started, "You know, that looks like . . . .no, it couldn't be."

"Yes it could," I said. "Look, there's a note on the windshield."

Everyone raced toward the van. Brad pulled the note from under the wiper blade and read it silently. A smile came over his face.

35

FACTS

1. The first major industry to develop in what is now West Virginia was the salt industry. The Indians, by following the bison, elk, deer, and other animals, found salt for their own needs. When they set up boiling pots, evaporated the water, and recovered the remaining salt, an industry began.

2. In 1775, Mary Ingles, an Indian captive, became the first European to take part in this industry.

3. John Haymond built the first salt furnace in 1809 at Bulltown.

4. Joseph and David Ruffner began producing salt in the Kanawha Salines field at Malden in 1808. They further developed the well drilling and casing process originated by Elisha Brooks.

5. Twenty-seven counties in the state can produce salt brine. This salt is mostly sodium chloride, hydrochloric acid, bleaching powder, calcium and other chemicals. Salt brine serves as the basis for some of the chemical industries in the Kanawha Valley.

6. Booker Taliaferro Washington (1856-1915) spent his childhood days in Malden, West Virginia. He was later employed in the Ruffner salt works and credits Mrs. Viola Ruffner for inspiring him to secure an education. In 1881, he established the first vocational school for Negroes in America at Tuskegee Institute in Alabama.

7. Geologists agree that the New River is the second oldest river in the world. It carved a fourteen-mile gorge through 330 million year-old Nuttall sandstone. The fifty-three miles designated as a National River include deserted mining towns, bridges, rock-strewn rapids, and sheer sandstone cliffs.

8. The New River Gorge Bridge in Fayette County is the western hemisphere's longest single arch steel bridge and the highest bridge east of the Mississippi River. It is 3,030 feet long and 876 feet high.

9. Bridge Day occurs in the fall of each year. The bridge is closed to traffic, as hundreds of daredevils using colorful nylon chutes jump from the bridge. In 1997, a dozen people set the world record for simultaneous jumps.

10. Rapid Ratings:

Class I	Easy
Class II	Small waves, a few large rocks
Class III	Numerous waves, high and irregular
Class IV	Difficult, powerful maneuvering required
Class V	Extremely difficult, long and violent; riverbed is dangerously obstructed

Chapter 4

A State is Born

Chelsea, Brad, and I sat around Grandma's white kitchen table with a road map of West Virginia spread in front of us. Brad used a highlighter to trace Route 52 from Welch to Williamson, Route 119 to Charleston, I-77 to Williamson, West Virginia and Pleasant City, Ohio. Next he marked I-70 and traced it to Wheeling.

"This looks like the best route to take," announced Brad after he drew a circle around Wheeling.

"Gee, how long will that take?" Chelsea asked.

"Probably six to seven hours," answered Brad, "and it is not an easy trip."

"Why not?" I inquired.

"Twisting, two-lane roads the first part of the trip," Brad remarked. "Remember this is not California with a lot of freeways."

"And you don't have eight lanes of traffic to fight," I quipped.

"Forget that; Wheeling is a really neat place. It was the second largest city in Virginia at the time of the Civil War. Richmond was first," said Chelsea.

"You're beginning to sound like Mom again," moaned Brad.

"But it's true," Chelsea continued. "The National Road went to Wheeling, Virginia, right up to the Ohio River. So they needed a bridge to the West. The Wheeling Suspension Bridge was the first bridge to cross the Ohio, the first long-span, wire-cable suspension bridge, and for many years it was the longest bridge in the world."

"I'm glad you got the 'history gene' and not me," Brad teased.

"That really ties in secret lore from the mountains," I muttered, thinking aloud.

"Are we going to search the bridge or Independence Hall?" asked Brad.

Chelsea and I answered at the same time, "Independence Hall."

"Since this is such a long trip, maybe we could stay overnight," suggested Brad.

"Do you think Mom would let us?" asked Chelsea.

"Ask Uncle Ron first," I said.

"Right," said Brad, "I think we can get him to go along with the idea. Mom is a different case."

"Let's go work on your Dad," I said to Chelsea.

"I'll go, too," Brad commented, "but Chelsea, you do all the talking."

"I just had an idea," said Chelsea stopping dead in her tracks. "Let's go on to Pittsburgh and spend the night with the Hunters. They're always inviting us up. They've been friends with Mom and Dad for years, so they would like that idea."

"What about me? I don't know the Hunters," I explained.

"We'll tell them you're the family pet. They'll understand," said Brad laughing.

"Brad," scolded Chelsea, "don't be so mean. I'm sure the Hunters will be glad to have you, Ginny."

"Ginny, I was just kidding. Chelsea will be the problem, but the Hunters already know that," said Brad.

"Knock it off!" Chelsea ordered. "Now get serious. Are you going to help us convince Dad or not?"

"You're in charge," nodded Brad. "Let the convincing begin."

Just as I expected. Uncle Ron was easy. It took two days of making rash promises to get Aunt Fran's blessing, but she finally came around.

Brad had contacted Sakura, Morgan, and Erik. They couldn't make an overnight trip with us, so they were going to do some investigating on their own. They planned to day-trip to Pt. Pleasant and would stay in touch by computer and cell phone. If either group found the missing horseshoe, contact was to be made immediately.

Early on Friday morning, we began to wind our way along a narrow two-lane road that pushed along the floor of many valleys. Steep mountains towered above us as we traveled through Iaeger, Hanover, Justice, Gilbert, Varney, Delbarton, and into Williamson. We passed many small communities where minute frame houses sat in straight rows. Chelsea explained these were old "coal camps" where miners once lived in company-owned houses. Once the coalfields were open to unions, miners were paid in legal money and did not need to live on property owned by the coal company. Many miners later bought these houses and refurbished them.

For the next four hours, memories filled my head. First, it was of Tony, Ronnie, Cathy, Ann, and bombs falling. Scary thoughts and feelings were coming back. I shuddered as I thought about the coal miners on Blair Mountain. I felt I was in a dream world when the car rolled onto the four-lane Route 119 toward Holden, Logan, and Chapmanville. I fingered the antique locket around my neck and opened it to see the pictures of Sadie and Devil Anse Hatfield. From past adventures to the present one, West Virginia has been fascinating. I was intrigued and excited about finding the golden horseshoe again, and I secretly enjoyed the neat things I was learning. Brad gave Chelsea a tough time about her sounding like Aunt Fran, but I liked it.

From Charleston, Sissonville, Ripley, Mineral Wells, Parkersburg to Williamstown, the land was different from the coalfields. It was much flatter and lighter in color. Small farms with large houses and barns nestled in the rolling hills along the interstate. There was little change in this agrarian terrain as we traveled into Ohio and back along I-70 to Wheeling, West Virginia. We crossed Wheeling Island, and the Ohio River then turned right on Main Street. We passed the Wheeling Suspension Bridge and turned left onto Market Street. Independence Hall, built as a federal Custom House in 1859, dominated the corner of this historical area.

"Why would you have a Custom House here?" I asked Chelsea.

Glad to share information, Chelsea responded, "The National Road, the Ohio River, and later railroads. But mostly, nails."

"Nails!" I exclaimed.

"Nails," Chelsea responded. "With iron ore and coal in huge quantities, foundries were built and they produced nails. People traveling west would stop in Wheeling and buy supplies, you know, food and stuff. Well, they bought lumber and nails to build rafts or crude flatboats. They loaded families and some livestock on board and floated down the Ohio. When they found a place they liked they would tear the boat or raft apart, saving the valuable nails of course, and use them to build homes."

"If you're giving out information, get it right. Don't forget the steamboats," Brad added.

"I was about to mention them, but I was rudely interrupted," sneered Chelsea.

"Pardon me, your highness," remarked Brad.

Chelsea continued, "Steamboats began moving people and goods

41

WV Independence Hall
(Custom House)

as early as 1811 on the Ohio River. Wheeling had all kinds of businesses: hat shops, bakeries, breweries, glass factories, potteries, tanneries, paper mills, a broom factory, a woolen mill, and of course, iron mills. Sea captains could pay customs here or in New Orleans."

A light came on in my head and I chattered excitedly. "The wagon, the Conestoga wagon at the museum. They were used along The National Road. Wheeling, before the Civil War, was like St. Louis, a gateway to the West."

"All right California," said Chelsea laughing. "You're catching on. But it wasn't just wagons. There were stagecoaches with passengers and mail to be carried. Like I said earlier, Wheeling was the second largest city in Virginia."

"History class is over for now," said Brad as he pulled into the parking lot behind a three-story building of Renaissance Revival architecture.

"Look at the size of those doors," I commented as we walked along the sidewalk to the front entrance. "The carving on them is so neat."

"Tricked you," Brad said. "Those are not wood; they're cast iron. They tried to make this building fireproof, so iron was used for columns, shutters, exterior doors, staircases, roofs, and beams."

"Who's sounding like Mom now?" taunted Chelsea.

"Hey," commented Brad, "I'm just giving Ginny a break from your constant talking. It's my good deed for the day."

We entered the first floor and stepped onto a blue and yellow tile floor in a post office vestibule. Corinthian style columns framed the tall window and numbered mailboxes. An antique chandelier consisting of metal branches tipped with gas burners hung from the high ceiling.

"What happened to the Custom House?" I asked.

"Second floor," answered Chelsea. "The first floor served as a Post Office."

A middle-aged man from behind the glass put down the crossword puzzle he was working and came to the window. "Good afternoon, folks. What can I do for you today?"

"We want to tour the building, if that's okay," replied Brad, extending his hand through the open window. "I'm Brad Brown. This is my sister, Chelsea, and my cousin, Ginny West."

"Glad to meet you young people; just call me Sam," he said smiling as he reached out to shake hands with each of us. "No charge, history is free here. Just come around the corner to your right and I'll meet you at the elevator."

Our footsteps echoed on the tile as we headed toward the elevator. The four of us filled the small compartment as it dropped slowly to the basement.

Sam explained, "The tour begins with a twenty-minute video about statehood. Take the elevator

Cast Iron Door

up to the third floor; it was the U. S. District Court Room, but statehood meetings were held there because of its size. Then come down to the second floor; custom offices were located there. You'll end up with me on the first floor. I'll answer any questions you might have and explain the exhibits."

"Thank you, sir," Brad said with a nod.

The room seemed to be about the size of two classrooms. Pictures of Wheeling during the late 1800s and early 1900s lined the left wall, showing many of the businesses Chelsea had talked about earlier. A giant TV screen was centered in front of the room and old church pews, about twenty in all, faced the TV. The wall on the right was bare and signs on the back wall pointed out restrooms.

"How do we turn on the video?" I asked.

Sam replied, "I'll turn it on as I go back up to the main floor. You may

Portion of Iron Staircase in Independence Hall

want to sit about three or four rows back. The picture will be clearer."

"Great, thank you," I replied.

Sam waved as he left the room. We heard a clicking noise and then the sound of the elevator going upward.

"We'll watch the video first," Chelsea began, "and then we'll search around the room for notes or clues. I just feel something is here."

"Hurry and sit down. The video is starting," said Brad.

For the next twenty minutes, I was amazed at how West Virginia became a state. I watched actors playing John S. Carlile, Waitman T. Willey, Francis H. Pierpont, and Arthur I. Boreman create a government. It seemed at the beginning of the Civil War, when Virginia seceded from the Union, the majority of people living in the western portion of the state wanted to stay in the Union. This caused many of the Union supporters to move into Ohio and Pennsylvania, but some stayed in the Wheeling area. John S. Carlile, a lawyer from Clarksburg, wanted to form a new state. Francis H. Pierpont, a Fairmont lawyer, thought it was illegal under the U. S. Constitution to form a new state from Virginia without Virginia's permission. So Pierpont helped to set up "The Restored State of Virginia." He was elected governor of this state and its capital was Wheeling; at the same time Richmond was the Confederate state capital of Virginia.

"Chelsea," I whispered, "these men would have been shot as traitors if the Confederacy had won the war."

44

"Gutsy, weren't they?" she responded. "A lot of their neighbors considered them traitors anyway. Their families were threatened, and things were really heating up. Once President Lincoln recognized them as a legitimate state, troops under General George B. McClellan were sent to give protection to the members of the Wheeling Conventions."

The delegates then wrote a new constitution and formally applied for statehood. Once Waitman T. Willey amended the statehood bill to provide for the gradual emancipation of slaves, the U. S. Senate passed it with a vote of 23 to 17. President Lincoln signed the bill December 31, 1862, and proclaimed West Virginia a state April 20, 1863. According to his proclamation Congress would admit West Virginia as the 35th state in sixty days.

The video ended and Chelsea bolted from her seat. "Brad," she said, "you check under the pews for a note or clues or whatever. Ginny, help me check out the pictures on the wall. There has got to be something here. I can feel it."

My head reeled with the information from the video. I tried to concentrate on the pictures of Wheeling but I kept thinking about the fight West Virginia had becoming a state. They wanted to be liberated from Virginia, but united to the national government. Maybe that's why Arthur I. Boreman, the first governor of the new state, had the words "liberty" and "union" added to the state seal.

"Nothing here," announced Brad as he rose from his knees.

"Same here," replied a despondent Chelsea. "I just knew . . . ."

"Maybe we'll find something upstairs," I offered. "You know everything happened in that room. I'm sure we'll have better luck there."

"You're right," Brad agreed. "Come on, Chelsea, let's try the third floor."

A brooding Chelsea followed Brad and me into the elevator. When the door opened we stepped into a stately courtroom with rows of tall arched windows. Four large columns dominated the spacious center of the room. A raised judge's podium, in front of an elegant fresco and flanked by arched doors, stood behind this colonnade. Wooden benches for spectators and jurors were six deep on both sides of the columned area. A richly polished wooden rail made a "U" shape from one side of the judge's work area, around the four columns, to the other side of this area. The afternoon sun spilled through the open shutters and bathed the wooden rail and floor in warm streaks of gold.

"Gold! The rail!" I shrieked. "Chelsea, the rail is shaped like a horseshoe."

Judge's Podium

"I know, I know. There has got to be a clue in here somewhere," she shouted. "Brad, check the benches on the left side. I'll take the ones on the right."

"I'll do the windows and the judge's podium. Wait, I'll go over the rail first," I sputtered.

We all three dropped to our knees and began searching. Brad and Chelsea crawled around and under benches while I felt around columns and peered under the rail. After thirty minutes, all we had were dirty knees.

"We're missing something," Chelsea insisted. "Maybe it's on the second floor."

"I haven't checked the judge's area yet," I remarked. "Give me a few more minutes."

"I'll give you a hand," said Brad moving toward the raised platform.

I pulled the large, high-backed leather chair away from the desk and crawled into the dark shadows. As I ran my hands along the bottom rim of the desk, I shrieked, "I've found something!"

Chelsea and Brad rushed toward me as I held up a slip of paper. "It's not even folded. It's to me," I gasped.

"What's it say?" Chelsea demanded breathlessly.

I read slowly, ***"This horseshoe is of wood, not the golden one you seek. Look in the corner of knowledge, for that you always keep." Look in the corner of knowledge."***

"Any ideas?" I asked.

Brad muttered, " The ***"corner of knowledge,"*** that's got to be the Cultural Center."

"Maybe not," quipped Chelsea. "Maybe it is in Welch, back at Grandma's. Maybe the ***"corner of knowledge"*** is in the coal bin, where we found the horseshoe."

"Gee," Brad said scratching his head. "I feel like we're back at square one. I guess I'll try to get Sakura on the phone and tell her about the latest clue. What do you think the chances are that Pt. Pleasant is the ***"corner of knowledge?"***

"Is there a real place called ***"Corner of Knowledge?"*** Is there a town in West Virginia named ***Corner***?" I asked Chelsea.

"Or it may be under us," Chelsea said.

"Oh, this should be good," Brad mocked.

"Francis Pierpont's office was on the second floor, in the southeast corner. Arthur Boreman used the same office before he moved to the first Capitol Building," Chelsea explained.

"But I thought this was the first Capitol Building for West Virginia. Now I'm really confused," I confessed.

"No, No," began Chelsea, "this was the Capitol for The Restored State of Virginia and the building where the statehood bill and West Virginia's Constitution was drafted. The first Capitol of the state of West Virginia was just a few blocks away on Eoff Street, in a building leased from Linsly Institute."

I suggested, "Maybe that building is the ***"corner of knowledge."***

Brad asked, "Is it still standing?"

"Sure is," Chelsea answered, "but I think we ought to check the corners in this building first."

Pointing toward the exit, Brad replied, "Lead on, ladies."

I clutched the note in my hand as we left the courtroom and started toward the elevator. Our footsteps echoed in the hallway of the empty third floor. Chelsea pushed the down button and the elevator doors opened immediately.

"Not many people visit this place, do they?" Chelsea said rhetorically.

"It's summer and the middle of the week," I said.

"And the Pirates are playing in Pittsburgh at the new stadium," said Brad. "Guess where my friends from WVU are? Not in Wheeling, that's for sure."

"The reward," said Chelsea looking at me and winking, "will be split only two ways."

The door opened, we exited, and turned right into a corner office. A marker pointed out the actual desk of Francis Pierpont but stated the horsehair sofa, ingrain carpet, and reclining chair were period furnishings. The gasolier was a reproduction but the mantle was original to the building. The high ceiling and cathedral style windows added openness and light to the room. We spent about fifteen minutes looking around the sparse office before ending our second floor search. Frustrated, we boarded the elevator and descended to the first floor.

Sam greeted us as the elevator door opened. "How do you like it so far?" he inquired.

"It's great," I answered. "Do you get many visitors?"

"Just a handful now and then in the summer," he said. "But once school starts, that's something else. Busloads of kids are in here every day."

"You seem to have a lot of maps on this floor. Do you know of any place in West Virginia called *Corner*?" asked Chelsea.

Sam knitted his brow and scratched his chin, "*Corner*, *Corner*, I can't think of any town by that name. But I do know something about an important corner. Check out this map, right over here."

We moved to the right toward an electronic map about the size and height of a ping-pong table. It showed the outline of pre-Civil War Virginia. He motioned for us to pick up the headsets. We heard again about West Virginia becoming a state, but more important how it arrived at its present-day borders. As we listened, small lights appeared to denote certain towns. At the end of the presentation, the existing state of West Virginia (as described in the Statehood Bill) was elevated six inches above present-day Virginia.

"Wow, that's really cool," said Chelsea.

Sam smiled and said, "Most people like it. But you mentioned "*Corner*" earlier. It's not named corner, but it's in the corner of the state and it has a corner stone." He pointed to the corner of Tucker and Grant Counties where West Virginia meets Maryland. "Lots of history there. Lord Fairfax had his land surveyed, some people say by George Washington, and had his boundary marker placed there in 1746. Long

48

before we were a country. That corner stone was used to establish the state boundaries of Maryland, Virginia, and Pennsylvania."

My eyes met Chelsea's and we both smiled. I glanced over at Brad and he nodded. I said, "I think we have found the *"corner of knowledge."* If the horseshoe isn't there, the clue to finding it will be."

Brad extended his hand to Sam and said, "Thank you, sir. You have been a tremendous help. I think we'll be on our way. Again, thank you."

"But you haven't heard the debate between Lincoln's cabinet members," sputtered Sam. "We've got a Civil War map that lights up just like this one and a copy of the statehood bill."

"We'll catch those another time," Chelsea promised. "But we need to drive on to Pittsburgh tonight."

A sense of rejection could be heard in Sam's voice when he said, "Only have four people all day, and everybody wants to go to Pittsburgh."

"Only four today, someone was here earlier?" I asked.

Sam replied, "Just a young fellow. All he was interested in was the courtroom on the third floor."

I pressed on, "Was he searching for a missing horseshoe?"

"He didn't say anything about a horseshoe," Sam responded with a perplexed look on his face.

"What did he look like?" Chelsea questioned. "Was he by any chance driving a gray pickup truck?"

"He just looked like a regular guy and I don't know what he was driving," Sam said sharply.

"I think you're letting your imagination get away from you," Brad whispered to Chelsea. "It's time to go."

Chelsea and I shook hands with Sam and thanked him for his help. Brad made comments about the outstanding work the West Virginia Independence Hall Foundation, Inc. had accomplished in restoring the building. Sam extended an invitation to us to come back at any time.

Once outside the building, Chelsea said, "He was here. I bet he left the note."

"He who?" asked Brad.

"The guy who tried to kill me," replied Chelsea.

"What a drama queen," moaned Brad as he slapped his forehead.

"I don't think he really tried to kill you," I added, "but he does seem to appear everywhere we find a clue."

49

"What if Sakura found a clue at Pt. Pleasant? How would you explain that?" asked Brad.

"I hadn't thought about that," I replied.

"Besides, we don't know if this is the same guy we encountered earlier or not," Brad stated. "Just chill out, okay."

"I am not a drama queen," Chelsea mumbled as she climbed into the backseat.

"Drop it, okay," Brad requested.

"Are we going to the corner stone place?" I asked.

Chelsea corrected, "It's called the Fairfax Stone and it is historical."

"I'm thinking about it," answered Brad. "I'll need to call Mom and Dad. It would change the route I was going to take, and it will take us longer to get home."

"They'll let us," said Chelsea with confidence.

"Then you make the call," Brad said passing the cell phone to Chelsea.

Chelsea was on the phone for the next thirty minutes. She called Aunt Fran and Uncle Ron and got permission for us to change our travel plans. She tried several times to reach Sakura, but was unsuccessful. She turned that task back to Brad.

We reached the Hunters' home about six thirty. It was in a middle class suburban neighborhood with wide sidewalks, flower gardens, and swimming pools. The Hunters had planned a barbeque and rented a movie they thought we might enjoy. Instead of watching the movie, we shared with them the information about our search for the missing horseshoe. They both agreed the Fairfax Stone might be significant to our hunt. Mr. Hunter was going over a map with Brad when Chelsea and I went to bed.

FACTS

1. Steamboats appeared on the Ohio River as early as 1811.

2. The National Road reached Wheeling in 1818 and connected it to the East. During the 1820s more than 8,500 freight wagons brought products to and from Wheeling across this road.

3. Wheeling became a "port of delivery" on the Ohio River in 1831, meaning merchants could pay their duties in Wheeling rather than in New Orleans, a "port of entry."

4. The Wheeling Suspension Bridge, built between 1846 and 1849, was an innovative design by Charles Ellet Jr. It is a National Civil Engineering Landmark and is considered the most significant pre-Civil War bridge in the United States.

5. The Baltimore and Ohio Railroad reached Wheeling and solidified the city's place as a transportation hub in 1853.

6. In 1854, the U. S. Congress appropriated $88,000 for a Custom House to be built in Wheeling, Virginia. Ammi B. Young, supervising architect of the U. S. Treasury, chose to follow a Renaissance Revival style widely used in public buildings during the 19th century.

7. The U. S. Custom House, now called West Virginia Independence Hall, is on the corner of 16th and Market Street. After many owners and changes, the West Virginia Independence Hall Foundation leased the property in 1964 and began restoration. In 1995 it was designated as a site on the Civil War Discovery Trail.

8. The West Virginia Division of Culture and History has been the facility's administrator since 1979. The Division maintains a permanent statehood exhibit as described in this chapter. Parking and admission are free.

9. John S. Carlile, Waitman T. Willey, Francis H. Pierpont, and Arthur I. Boreman are accurately portrayed in this chapter concerning the statehood of West Virginia.

Chapter 5

Corner of Knowledge

The Hunters waved good-bye from their driveway as Brad backed the van cautiously into the street. He switched on the headlights and Chelsea loaded the CD player with five of her favorite discs. I snuggled down in the back seat and prepared for a nap.

"Hey, Bro, which way are we going?" Chelsea asked.

Brad answered, "By way of Pennsylvania, West Virginia, Maryland, and back to West Virginia."

Coming to a sitting position, I said, "Whoa, how long is that going to take?"

"It really won't be all that long. Maybe two and one half hours," Brad replied.

"Let me guess," said Chelsea looking at the map. "We're going to take I-79 to Morgantown and then I-68 to Maryland. At Friendsville, we take 42 and then follow state Route 219 back into West Virginia."

"You're getting better at this," said Brad. "But I want to stay on I-68 over to Route 219. I think the road will be better."

Peering over Chelsea's shoulder to see the map, I remarked, "I think we might have a problem. I can see Route 219 but there is no road on this map that goes to the Fairfax Stone."

Brad chuckled, "Mr. Hunter told me last night that a historical marker on 219 will direct us to the cornerstone. He said we would be on a gravel road for a little more than two miles."

"The road is not even paved! How historical did you say this was?" I taunted Chelsea.

"Very," she responded. "We may not do things show-biz style like they do in California, but this is significant."

"If you say so," I sighed and stretched out on the back seat.

When I opened my eyes, we were at the top of a hill and ready to climb an even higher hill. This narrow two-lane road was like a roller coaster with old houses and buildings stacked on the sides of converging mountains. Crammed next to the road were many small cafes advertising food, such as pizza, subs, beer, and cappuccino.

"Where are we?" I asked.

"Morgantown," answered Brad. "You're seeing the back streets. I'm taking a shortcut to I-68."

"I can't believe people park cars on these hills and leave them," I gasped seeing automobiles parked at forty-five degree angles with their wheels turned into the curb.

"A good emergency brake is a high priority up here," laughed Brad.

"We were in farm country and now we're in mountains," I exclaimed.

Chelsea replied, "We get a lot out of these mountains. In the southern part of the state you have coal and natural gas. There is salt brine and oil in the middle of the state. No one knew about the oil until they started drilling a salt well and struck oil instead. Up here there is a lot of clay, limestone, and gravel. That's why the glass industry and cement and block businesses are in this area. Oh, and the logging industry, I almost forgot about it. With all the forest land. . . . "

"Give us a break," said Brad rolling his eyes. "Next you'll be giving us pop quizzes."

"Not every state is as unusual as West Virginia," insisted Chelsea.

"California has many land uses and its topography is very diverse," I announced.

"Yes," Chelsea said, "and California stretches almost the entire length of the west coast. West Virginia is small and landlocked."

I thought about what Chelsea had said as we traveled away from the interstate and along the crest of mountain ridges. On Route 52 dump trucks loaded with coal were dominant. In the New River Gorge area, flatbed trucks hauling lumber prevailed. Here, trucks carrying gravel, sand, and cinderblocks took possession of the narrow two-lane roads. Occasionally, limestone and sandstone quarries came into view, but this particular corner of West Virginia seemed secluded from the rest of the state.

Soon after we passed Silver Lake Park, Chelsea shouted, "That's it. That's the marker. We turn left about a mile down 219."

I leaned forward between the bucket seats. I had no idea what to expect when Brad turned left onto a gravel road. The one-lane road cut a wide path through high weeds, pine trees, and shrubs. The white dust from the gravel formed a small cloud around the van as we headed toward a grassy meadow. Ahead, yellow and white wild flowers sprinkled with tiny pink sunbursts danced on nature's remote stage. The road ended about twenty-five feet from a large oak tree that appeared to be guarding a small obelisk and a table-sized flat stone. I wondered if this could be the *"corner of knowledge."*

Jumping out of the car, Chelsea announced, "We're here. Come on."

The historical marker told how Lord Thomas Fairfax had his property resurveyed in 1746 to reaffirm the original grant of land given by King Charles II in 1669. A stone with the letters FX and the date 1746 was placed at the headwaters of the North Branch of the Potomac River to mark the claim.

I noticed the obelisk had an FX and the number 46 carved into it. The 17 had been chipped away. About five feet from this small monument lay the Fairfax Stone. It was resting in a shallow creek bed with a small stream of water, the source of the North Branch of the Potomac, trickling out of its base. A rock wall of time-worn sandstone opened its arms around this massive marker. Chelsea, Brad, and I were able to stand on the stone with plenty of room to spare.

"This doesn't look like a *"corner of knowledge"* to me," I said. "In fact, it doesn't look like any kind of corner."

"It's definitely a corner," said Brad. "It's the corner of Grant and Tucker Counties and the corner of West Virginia and Maryland."

"It was used to locate the Mason-Dixon line and settle a dispute between Pennsylvania and Virginia," added Chelsea as her eyes scanned the area. "Where would you hide a clue out here?"

"I'll search the creek bed and around the edge of the stone," offered Brad.

"You take the wall and I'll take the tree and small stone," I said to Chelsea.

She replied, "Let's do it."

The small stone monument was easily examined. It sat alone and the grass around it had been trimmed. It didn't take long to realize nothing was hidden there. I moved toward the tree and saw for the first time that a trashcan, made from an empty oil drum, sat behind it. The container

54

Fairfax Marker and Stone

was filled with discarded picnic supplies and a generous amount of empty beer cans.

"Oh, no," I moaned, "I may need some help over here."

Chelsea asked, "What's up?"

"There's a can spilling over with trash back here. Should I go through the whole thing?"

"Probably not," Brad shouted. "The notes so far have been on the surface of things. Whoever is leaving them wants them to be found. Just check the top layer."

Chelsea by this time had joined me at the tree. "He's referring to my assassin. You know, the guy in the gray truck that disappears every time we find a message."

Chelsea and I spent all of five minutes picking through the trash and agreed there was nothing there. Brad joined us and admitted he found nothing in or around the creek bed.

"So much for the "corner of knowledge," he remarked. "Let's head for home."

"It really seemed like a good idea," muttered Chelsea.

"What corner do we look in now?" I asked as we headed for the van.

"Beats me," Brad replied. "Maybe Sakura and company have had better luck."

"I doubt that," Chelsea quipped, "or we would have heard from them by now."

We climbed into the van, buckled up and drove back to 219. At Thomas we got on Route 32 traveling south. The area appeared to be sparsely populated. Just a few homes and a turkey farm could be seen from the highway. Signs for several ski resorts, Dolly Sods, and Seneca Caverns welcomed tourists to experience wild, wonderful West Virginia. Once we entered state Route 33, going toward Elkins and Buckhannon, traffic picked up. Fast food restaurants appeared on both sides of the road. I chuckled to myself as I thought of my brother David. He always called these areas "French Fry Alley." We stopped and had a few burgers before we got on I-79. We passed Stonewall Jackson Lake, Burnsville Lake, and Sutton Lake as we rode toward Charleston.

"Why didn't we take Route 19?" Chelsea asked. "It's more direct."

"I know. I just thought we might stop in Charleston and see Sakura. I still haven't been able to reach her," replied Brad in a somber tone.

"Getting worried, are you?" teased Chelsea as she winked at me.

"Not at all," Brad assured her. "I'm just trying to be hospitable. Why don't you give me a hand? Dial this number and see if they can meet us somewhere."

"Say please," Chelsea taunted.

"Please," he said with a piercing look.

Chelsea took the cell phone and tried to reach Sakura. She was ready to give up on the fifth attempt when Morgan answered the phone.

We heard Chelsea's side of the conversation as she said, "Where have you guys been? We found a note in Wheeling telling us to search the *"corner of knowledge."* So we go to the state's nearest corner, the Fairfax Stone, but found nothing. You did? Where? What did it say? Can you meet us at the clown's place on MacCorkle Avenue? You know, Exit 95, the one near the turnpike entrance. . . . Okay, see you in about an hour. Bye."

Chelsea chattered excitedly, "They found a note in Pt. Pleasant. Morgan didn't tell me what it said, but they will bring it with them. She said Erik was spun up about UFOs and a moth man. I have no idea what that is about. Oh, there was also something about an Indian curse."

"Where was Sakura? Why didn't she answer the phone?" questioned Brad.

"Did they see any real Indians?" I asked.

"I can't answer those questions. You'll have to ask them," said Chelsea. "A little worried about Cherry Blossom, hey Bro."

Brad scowled and snapped, "Just mind your own business, okay."

56

Chelsea raised her eyebrows and looked back at me. I signaled for her to be quiet. We rode in silence for the next thirty minutes. I didn't know what Brad was worried about, but I was eager to hear about this moth man and an Indian curse.

As we turned onto the exit ramp for MacCorkle Avenue, I spotted Sakura's Jeep in the parking lot of McDonald's. "They're already here, good," I announced.

Brad parked the van next to the Jeep and hurried toward the entrance without waiting for Chelsea and me.

"Boy, is he ever in a hurry," Chelsea whispered to me.

"I think he really likes Sakura. You had better back off," I warned.

"Maybe, but he's my brother. I've got to rag on him some or it wouldn't be natural," she responded.

Morgan met us at the door. "Hey guys, glad you made it. We're over here," she said motioning toward a rounded booth in the back. "We've already picked up some drinks and snacks."

Brad and Sakura were sitting close and talking intently to each other. Erik jumped up and spread his arm to show off the wild looking t-shirt he was wearing. It was black with a picture of a man's body between two massive yellow wings. The body had gray, scaly skin, and the wings appeared to be folded back. The eyes were almost as large as his head and were bright red. Whirls of neon colors seemed to erupt from the creature in all directions. Erik turned so we could view the back of the shirt. It was solid black with an Internet address in iridescent yellow, "http://www. mothmanlives.com."

"Check it out," said Erik as he turned slowly in place.

"A relative of yours?" asked Chelsea laughing.

"No, a real creature. He was first spotted in 1966 at Point Pleasant. He's still there. People are just afraid to come forward," explained Erik.

Morgan moaned, "Oh, Erik, it was a bird, probably a crane. That particular area was and still is a bird sanctuary. A lot of the people who saw this thing were out there just to party hearty."

"Says you," Erik remarked. "This remote area was home to an Ordnance Works during World War II. They produced TNT (tri-nitro-toluene) a highly dangerous material used in wartime explosives. They stored these explosives in underground bunkers made of cement and steel and camouflaged with dirt so they wouldn't be spotted from the air."

I asked, "What does that have to do with this moth man?"

Erik explained with a straight face, "This is where the creature lives. He might be an experiment gone wrong or a mutant mad scientist who breathed in too many toxic fumes."

"Like my brother, Erik," said Morgan.

"Okay, go ahead and laugh. I saw the movie. Something is out there," Erik replied.

"Does a movie make it real?" Chelsea asked.

"Sakura believes it," Erik persisted. "She wouldn't have driven us out there if she didn't."

"She was just being kind, you know, to dumb animals," teased Morgan.

"Shot down twice in the same day. Ladies, you are too hard on me," said Erik.

"What do you mean twice?" I asked.

"Cornstalk's curse," Erik began.

This caught Brad's attention and he looked up and asked, "What about it?"

"This one is mine," said Morgan. " We visited Tu-Endie-Wei State Park. That's where the Battle of Pt. Pleasant took place. The park has all kinds of neat things, several monuments, a marker left by a French explorer, and the Mansion House Museum. The house is really a log cabin. Would you believe we saw a flower arrangement made from Anne Bailey's hair. They even had furniture over 150 years old."

"The curse," interrupted Brad.

"Oh, there really wasn't any. The idea of a curse was written into a play about Chief Cornstalk in the early 1900s. It was added

Point Pleasant
Battle Monument

58

Mansion House Museum in Tu-Endie-Wei Park

for drama. But I must admit he had a right to put a curse on the town. He was trying to warn the townspeople about an upcoming Indian attack when he, his son, and Red Hawk were murdered," Morgan explained.

"Are you sure?" Brad asked. "A lot of people believed in that curse. They even blamed the collapse of the Silver Bridge on it."

"And many other things," Sakura broke in. "The park ranger explained all of this to us at great length. He also lives near the McClintic Wildlife Preserve, or the TNT area as the locals call it."

"Myths," said Morgan as she spread her arms and showed empty palms turned upward.

"What's a guy to do?" Erik shrugged. "The mystery is all gone."

"But you found a note, didn't you? Please tell us that is for real," I implored.

Almost jumping out of her seat, Sakura said, "Oh, yes, the note is real. It had my name on it." She rummaged in her purse and handed a folded sheet of paper to Brad.

Brad unfolded the note and read aloud, "*'Come to the mountains to rest, enjoy well prepared food, before completing your quest.'* Back to the mountains, but we've been in the mountains."

"Back up," I said. "I don't have this *"corner of knowledge"* being in Pt. Pleasant figured out yet."

"Me neither," Chelsea chimed in. "We were in the corner of the state, but you found the note in Pt. Pleasant. What gives?"

"'Tu-endie-wei' is a Wyandotte Indian phrase that means the "point

59

Chief Cornstalk Monument

between two waters." The point, which is like a corner, is where the Kanawha and Ohio Rivers meet," Sakura explained.

"Yeah," Morgan interrupted. "The Mansion House sits in the corner of the point and that's where we found the note. It was in the corner on the third floor."

"There was a cramped root cellar/kitchen that was mostly underground. The main floor had a parlor and dining room that would easily fit inside our great room," said Erik. "There were two bedrooms on the second floor with beds so short I would never have been able to stretch out. Then you climbed into a loft area that housed a museum."

"There were old tools, buttons, pictures, and dresses on display. I had bent down to examine some handmade nails near the end of a glass display case, and there was the note," Sakura said.

"And the best part," Morgan began, "was the gray truck. I saw it parked next to the flood wall when we came out."

Chelsea's eyes grew large when she asked, "Did you see anyone in it? Are you sure it was the one that's been following us?"

"Or leading us," Erik replied. "I'm sure, it was the same one."

"We didn't see anyone around the truck. I don't know if it was there when we arrived, but we did see it when we left," Sakura assured Chelsea.

"Now don't blow anything out of proportion," Brad said to Chelsea. "I think maybe, just maybe, this guy might be leaving the notes. But he isn't out to harm you or anyone else."

"That's easy for you to say," said Chelsea. "No one tried to run you down."

We all began talking at once trying to assure Chelsea she was safe. We finally agreed with Brad's conclusion that the stranger was involved with the notes.

"Where to next?" Erik asked.

"To the mountains to rest and eat," I answered.

"That narrows it to about fifty places," said Brad as he pulled the folded map out of his pocket.

Chelsea, without looking at the map, began naming parks, "Pipestem, Babcock, Watoga, Twin Falls, Bluestone, Blackwater Falls, Cacapon—all of these places are in the mountains and have cabins, rooms and food available."

Erik asked, "Does it have to be a state park?"

"No, it doesn't have to be," Brad answered.

"Don't forget, *well prepared food,*" I reminded them.

"The Bavarian Inn is in Shepherdstown and it is known for good food," said Morgan.

"The General Lewis Inn is in Lewisburg, and I remember having great waffles there," Chelsea remarked.

"What about the Greenbrier Hotel? It's in the mountains and is known for it's great food and a cooking school," I added.

"That's a good possibility. This note is so puzzling," Brad muttered.

"The Greenbrier would be a wonderful place to visit," said Sakura smiling at Brad.

"We could take in the bunker, now that it's open to the public," agreed Brad.

"What bunker? Like the TNT place?" Erik asked.

"Oh, no, explosive materials were never stored there. This bunker was built during the Cold War as an underground fallout shelter. It was suppose to house the members of Congress and their aides in the event of a nuclear attack. A hospital was also built underground."

"I didn't know that," I gasped.

"Stick around, California, you've got a lot to learn," Chelsea quipped.

"You can really tour this place?" Erik questioned.

"Only on certain days," said Brad. "Let me check this out and I'll get back in touch with you."

"Can we do this in a day?" asked Morgan.

"Yes," replied Sakura. Looking at Brad, she continued, "I'm very eager to go."

"Just remember to leave the cell phone on this time," he whispered to her.

Morgan remarked to Chelsea, "The Greenbrier is so exclusive. What are you going to wear?"

"No pants," Chelsea answered. "I'll let Mom call this one."

"Be sure to let me know," Morgan said.

"I think I'll wear pants, long ones," said Erik winking at Brad.

We all laughed and said our good-byes. Erik and Morgan walked Chelsea and me back to the van. We pretended not to be watching as Chelsea used the side mirror to give us a detailed description of Brad and Sakura holding hands and stealing a quick kiss. Erik and Morgan left immediately when Sakura called them. Brad, in a much better mood now, joined us in the van.

"Ready to go home?" he asked.

"Ready," we said in unison.

I was up front now and Chelsea stretched out in the back seat. I made small talk with Brad for a while, but I was beginning to nod off by the time we got to Bender's Bridge.

"Ginny," said Brad, "go ahead and sleep. I'm okay. I never get sleepy when I'm driving."

"Thanks," I mumbled as I adjusted a pillow against the door.

FACTS

1. Fairfax Lands: Five million acres in northern Virginia were given to a group of court favorites by King Charles II in 1669. The land was then sold and eventually inherited by Thomas, the sixth Lord Fairfax. In 1733 he petitioned King George II to reaffirm his land title. It was not until 1746 that the surveyors found and marked the point at the source of the North Branch of the Potomac River. At that point they placed a stone marked "FX." This stone later helped in determining the borders of Virginia, West Virginia, and Maryland.

2. After the American Revolution, the English system of land ownership was abolished by Virginia. The courts agreed that other land claimers had more right to the land than the Fairfax heirs.

3. West Virginia borders: The entire western border is one of rivers. The Ohio, Big Sandy, and Tug Fork separate the state from Ohio, Kentucky and part of Virginia. The southern and eastern borders are principally formed by the ridges of the Allegheny Mountains. The northern border of the Eastern Panhandle between Maryland and West Virginia is completely shaped by the Potomac River. There are five straight-line border sections of the state. The Fairfax Stone was confirmed as the starting point of the Maryland-West Virginia border in the United States Supreme Court in 1912. After the American Revolution, Pennsylvania and Virginia agreed to extend the east-west part of the Mason-Dixon Line by five degrees. The line that created the Northern Panhandle ran due north until it intercepted the Ohio River.

4. Celoron de Blainville, a French explorer, buried a leaden plate in 1749 at the confluence of the Ohio and Kanawha Rivers, claiming the land for France.

5. Anne Bailey, an Indian fighter, took over for her husband after he was killed during the Battle of Pt. Pleasant. She later saved Fort Lee by riding 200 miles roundtrip to get gunpowder. When the frontier moved westward, she became a mail carrier.

6. Battle of Pt. Pleasant was fought on October 10, 1774. Colonel Andrew Lewis's 1,100 Virginia militiamen decisively defeated

a like number of Indians led by Shawnee Chieftain Cornstalk. This is considered to be the first battle of the American Revolution because it broke the power of the Indians in the Ohio Valley and prevented an alliance between the British and Indians.

7. Lord Dunmore was named governor of Virginia in 1771. He appointed Colonel Andrew Lewis, a veteran of the French and Indian Wars as commander of the Virginia troops. By getting them to fight the Indians, Dunmore, a Tory, hoped to divert Virginians from the trouble brewing with England.

8. Chief Cornstalk had befriended the settlers after the Battle of Point Pleasant. He traveled to Fort Randolph to warn Captain Arbuckle of a possible Indian attack. Afraid of a trick, Arbuckle ordered Cornstalk and his companion, Red Hawk, held prisoner. Cornstalk's son, Elinipsico, was also held captive when he went to see what had happened to his father. The next day two soldiers from the fort were killed by a renegade band of Indians. Believing these Indians were trying to rescue Cornstalk, soldiers opened fire on the prisoners and killed all three.

9. On December 15, 1967, just after 5:00 p.m., the Silver Bridge spanning the Ohio River between Point Pleasant and Kanauga, Ohio, collapsed, killing forty-six people. Some attributed this disaster, as well as many fires and floods, to be the result of Cornstalk's Curse. There is no historical accounting of such a curse. There was a play written about Cornstalk in which he uttered a curse, but this was to enhance drama.

10. In the mid-1960s there were reported sightings of a man/bird creature in an area six miles north of Point Pleasant. This area, now known as the McClintic Wildlife Preserve, was used to store wartime explosives during World War II. For the next thirteen months, reports came in to police about television and radio interference, animal mutilations, pets disappearing, etc. and climaxed with the collapse of the Silver Bridge. Some locals explain the events by telling of a "moth-man" or the curse of Cornstalk. Most scientists think the creature sighted was a mutant strain of the "sandhill crane."

Chapter 6

Deep in the Mountains

On the following Wednesday we left Welch around 9:00 a.m. traveling Route 16 through Pineville, Mullens, Sophia, and into Mabscott. We were on the West Virginia Turnpike for a short distance before taking I-64 toward White Sulphur Springs. Interstate 64 seemed vast as it opened into six lanes of traffic. This was easier traveling than the curvy two lanes we had followed earlier. We passed exits for East Beckley, Grandview Park, Beaver, an airport, and Shady Spring. From here the road narrowed to four lanes and traffic became sparse. The mountainous terrain lifted us above the small towns named on the exit signs. My ears began to fill with fluid when we crested Sandstone Mountain. I swallowed several times trying to relieve the pressure. As we started down the mountain, I spotted a semi-truck half way up a runaway ramp. I guess he hadn't heeded the yellow warning signs about steep grades. The Historical District of Hinton was designated as Exit 139 and the New River came into view.

It seemed I was spending my summer in a car riding around West Virginia. It wouldn't be so bad if Eric were here. We couldn't get reservations at the same time to tour the bunker in the Greenbrier Hotel. Sakura, Morgan, and Eric were taking the 1:15 tour so they were ahead of us, somewhere on the road. We were scheduled for the 2:00 group and planned to meet with them later in Beckley. I was looking forward to seeing Eric this afternoon.

"Check out the name of this bridge," Chelsea said, pulling me away from my daydreaming and into the real world.

"The marker calls it the Mary Draper Ingles Bridge. Was she some distant relative?" I asked.

"No," Chelsea answered. Sounding like Aunt Fran, she continued, "Her family was massacred by Indians and she was captured. She escaped and traveled along this route to get back East. The trail she followed is marked by. . . ."

"I see we're back to West Virginia History 101," Brad interjected.

"Just making intelligent conversation," Chelsea snapped.

"Hey, there's a sign for Green Sulphur Springs. Just how many sulphur springs do you have in this area?" I asked.

"You'd better take this one, Great Knowledgeable Sister," Brad teased looking at Chelsea.

"I'm so glad you realize who has the brains in the family," said Chelsea. She continued, "This part of the state and the eastern panhandle has Blue, Green, Red, Yellow, and White Sulphur Springs. Then there are Mineral, Berkeley, Capon, Salt Sulphur, Sweet, Dunmore, and Minnehaha. Gee, I know there are more. I just can't remember all of them."

"Why are they only in this part of the state?" I asked.

Brad moaned, "I can't believe you asked. Do you really want to hear all this?"

Chelsea quipped, "Because of the Allegheny Range of the Appalachian Mountains. They are old, really old. We're talking dinosaur age here."

"I don't get it. What do the mountains have to do with the springs?" I asked.

"It took millions of years of uplift and erosion in these mountains for salt, sulphur and iron to filter through cracks of bedrock. Then pressure, from deep inside the earth, caused the water to bubble to the surface. That's what created the springs." Chelsea explained.

"Oh," I replied feeling dumb. "I do remember something like that from Earth Science."

Chelsea continued, "Some of the springs are even warm. Hey, they've been major tourist attractions forever. Even the Indians realized these springs had healing powers."

"Wow," was all I could say. I was constantly being overwhelmed with this state. I racked my brain to come up with something comparable from my home state of California, but I couldn't think of anything.

We continued to cross mountains as exit signs for Sam Black Church, Rupert, Alta, Alderson and Pence Springs (she had forgotten one) indicated off ramps, leading to small communities. Ahead I saw an exit sign for Lewisburg and Ronceverte.

Chelsea turned sideways in the front seat and said, "Ron. . . ."

"Get ready for another lecture," interrupted Brad, making eye contact with me through the rearview mirror.

"Never mind," exclaimed Chelsea as she turned forward and began to pout.

"Ignore him," I pleaded. "Chelsea, I like the things you're telling me. All of this is new and interesting to me."

Chelsea, with a big smile on her face said to Brad, "See, other people, especially intelligent ones, appreciate me."

Brad rolled his eyes and said, "Talk on, motor mouth."

Chelsea turned and began, "I was going to tell about Ronceverte. The word is French, translated it means bramble or thick green briers. This area was covered with them."

"French or brambles?" I asked.

"Both," replied Chelsea. "The French did a lot of fur trapping and trading in this area."

"My turn for show and tell," announced Brad as he abruptly exited I-64 and turned toward Lewisburg and Route 60.

"Just where do you think you're going?" demanded Chelsea. "We need to get to White Sulphur Springs."

"All in due time, little sister. I'm taking you children to a place where you can "enjoy well prepared food, before completing your quest," Brad answered. "You do remember the note and why we are here? Well, don't you?"

" Fort Savannah!" I exclaimed when a large motel with a log cabin restaurant bearing the sign "Fort Savannah" appeared.

"That was the original name of Lewisburg. General Andrew Lewis, you know, the Indian fighter at Pt. Pleasant, built Fort Savannah on this site in 1755. He was the commander of the fort when he assembled troops to fight Cornstalk. I know a little about the state," said Brad as he gave Chelsea a condescending look.

We followed Route 60 through the town of Lewisburg. Restored buildings, antique shops, and antebellum homes sat quietly on tree-lined streets. Numbered historical markers used for walking tours were plentiful. Brad turned left on East Washington Street and an antique stage coach, sitting under a canopy in front of a huge two-story white house, came into view. The sign out front read: "The General Lewis Inn."

"How old is this place?" I asked.

Brad answered, "Not as old as General Andrew Lewis. This place and the town were named after him, but John Withrow built this house in 1834. It's a popular inn and restaurant now. Let's have lunch!"

The General Lewis Inn

Brad parked his Camry in the circular driveway. We hurried over to take a look at the antique stagecoach. A marker stated the old coach transported guests between the many mineral springs in the area across the James River and Kanawha Turnpike (now U.S. Route 60). We left the coach and crossed the long shaded veranda dotted with rocking chairs. We entered the Inn and were greeted by a receptionist at the front desk. Here another marker identified the hand built walnut and pine desk as being used in the Sweet Chalybeate Springs Hotel as early as 1760. Thomas Jefferson and Patrick Henry had registered at this desk.

"Mom would love this place," Chelsea whispered to me as Brad inquired about lunch. "Look at all the antiques."

"I've never seen so much stuff," I commented as my eyes scanned the walls of a narrow hallway to the left of the desk. Handmade utensils, musical instruments and all sorts of tools hung from the floor to the ceiling.

"We're in luck," Brad announced. "Follow me."

We followed Brad through a cozy sitting room with exposed hand-hewn beams. The room was furnished with rustic rocking chairs, settees, a library table and a corner cupboard. Although it was mid-summer, a small fire smoldered in the fireplace. We passed through another doorway into the dining room. Tables covered in white cloths and adorned with calico napkins, sat amidst antique chairs. Cupboards and windowsills held an array of old fashioned china pieces and saltcellars. We were seated near a front window, giving us a view of the surrounding homes.

"This is neat," I said looking at Brad.

Brad replied, "I thought you might like it."

"Well I don't," Chelsea announced. "I bet Sakura, Morgan, and Eric are eating in the café at the Greenbrier."

"I hope so," commented Brad. "That was the plan."

Chelsea demanded, "What plan?"

"Rest and good food, remember. The horseshoe could be here just as well as at the Greenbrier," Brad explained.

"Well, I think. . . . " Chelsea began.

"He's right, Chelsea," I said defending Brad.

"It didn't take you long to change sides," snapped Chelsea.

The waitress approached the table and asked if we were ready to order. Although the menu featured fried chicken, country ham, and other southern dinners, we chose pork barbeque sandwiches with French fries.

"Did you notice the sign on the reception desk about ghost tours?" I asked Chelsea attempting to cheer her up.

"Yeah," she answered flatly.

"They start here," Brad remarked. "In fact, one of the rooms here is supposed to have a ghost."

"I'm not interested unless he has a horseshoe," grumbled Chelsea. "I think we should be at the Greenbrier."

"We have a team, remember," Brad scolded. "They are checking out the Greenbrier proper while we're investigating the General Lewis Inn. Both teams will go through the bunker."

"That's another thing," Chelsea began. "Why are we going to the bunker? I want to see the Greenbrier Hotel."

"The horseshoe is more likely to be in the bunker than the hotel," I stated.

"How did you figure that?" asked Chelsea.

Brad answered, "Twofold. First, the bunker is deep in the mountain and second, the Culinary School is located inside the bunker."

"Oh," Chelsea replied. "I hadn't thought of that."

The waitress appeared with plates piled high with crisp French fries and homemade barbeque. She placed tall glasses of fresh lemonade in front of us and promised to return with the dessert menu.

"What do you know about the ghost?" I asked Brad between bites of food.

"Is it General Lewis?" Chelsea questioned.

"No, this ghost is from the Civil War," Brad explained. "A major battle was fought in Lewisburg in May of 1862. In fact, the 8th Virginia Cavalry along with its artillery was placed in reserve behind the Withrow house (General Lewis Inn). When the Confederate left collapsed, the 44th Ohio Union troops stormed the artillery. The gunners fought bravely, but never had a chance. At least twenty soldiers died in the back yard and many were wounded. The ghost is from that battle."

"Who won?" I asked.

"The Union troops took control of Lewisburg. Ninety-five Confederate soldiers were killed and hundreds were wounded. The John Wesley Methodist Church, the Old Stone Presbyterian Church, and the Greenbrier County Library were used as hospitals." Brad continued, "If only we had more time, we could go by those places today. Soldiers scratched their names on the hospital walls. You can see some of the names in the old library."

"I didn't know that," Chelsea said. "I can't believe this little place has so much history."

"There are some things you don't know. Big shock isn't it?" teased Brad.

"Now I wish we weren't in a hurry to get to the bunker," I moaned.

"Same here," Chelsea agreed. "Hey, maybe we can come back here and spend a day or two. Wouldn't it be neat to stay in the ghost room!

"About 200 acres with more than 60 structures and battle sites from the Revolutionary and Civil Wars make Lewisburg a paradise for history buffs," said the waitress as she handed us dessert menus. "I didn't mean to interrupt, but I couldn't help overhearing your conversation. I'll check back with you in a few minutes to see if you would like anything else."

"Talk about a ghost," Chelsea muttered. "Did you hear her walk up?"

"No," I whispered as a shiver ran up my spine.

Brad announced, "I'm stuffed, but if you guys want dessert, we have time to order."

"None for me," I said.

"Let's hit the road," Chelsea suggested.

Brad paid the bill and we started to leave the Inn.

Chelsea paused on the veranda and looked up and down the road.

"Expecting someone?" asked Brad.

"Yeah, a gray truck," Chelsea quipped.

"There may be a note on the windshield," I hinted as we hurried toward the car.

After reaching the Camry, Brad remarked, "No note, no horseshoe, and no truck. Three strikes, we're out of here. Let's go."

We piled into the Camry and followed the circular driveway onto Route 60 to travel the nine miles to White Sulphur Springs. The narrow road twisted around farms and between antique shops. A sign advertising "Greenbrier Bunker Tour" directed us to the back of an abandoned high school. A serious looking young man dressed in khaki pants with a dark green shirt and white Greenbrier nametag stood next to an open door.

"This must be the place," Brad remarked.

"It's about ten minutes until two. You made good time, Bro," Chelsea commented.

Brad parked under a huge maple tree across from the vacant school. Brick homes dominated one side of the street and a church sat on the corner. A line of six people formed near the uniformed man. Brad and I followed Chelsea as she crossed the street and headed toward the door. The young man nodded as we entered the building. About twelve people were crowded around a cafeteria table with money in hand as a middle-aged woman read names from a clipboard. Brad removed a check from his wallet and joined the others near the table.

"I guess it's a good thing we made reservations," I said.

"Mom always thinks of stuff like that," Chelsea said.

We overheard the woman behind the table tell a group of twelve people from Virginia that she would add another tour bus, but they would not be leaving until 2:45. They agreed this would be fine since they did not want to split up. She spoke with Brad next. He handed her the check, she scratched a name off the list, and handed him a slip of paper. With a smile on his face, he walked back toward us.

"All set," he announced. "The bus will pick us up in about two minutes right outside the door."

We left the building to join the line. Just then a dark green bus turned the corner and people began climbing out of cars. When the bus stopped, over twenty people had joined us in line. The uniformed man moved into the street, motioned for us to follow, and directed us to the door of the bus.

With a soft-pitched tone and a heavy southern accent, he said, "Please show your ticket as you enter and fill the bus from the back to the front."

When I passed this young man, I noticed his nametag read "Robert Moore." He appeared to be in his late thirties, of thin build, with collar-length dark hair that wanted to curl. His expression never changed as he checked each ticket. When everyone had boarded, he climbed on the bus and counted the passengers. He nodded to the driver and we started to move as the bus lurched forward.

I nudged Chelsea and whispered, "I hope this is as much fun as the last bus ride we had."

She giggled and nodded as the guide from the Greenbrier braced himself in front of the bus.

"Good afternoon, I'm Robert Moore," he said. "I will be your guide for the bunker tour. I am retired from the U. S. Air Force having served in intelligence the last eight years of a twenty-year career. Your ride to the bunker, sometimes called the Eisenhower Bunker, will be a short one. We will pass the Greenbrier Resort on the right and climb a small hill. The building you now see on the right is the West Virginia Wing of the Greenbrier. It sits about sixty feet from Route 60. The bunker is hidden under that wing. The stables you see on the left belong to the Greenbrier. When the bunker was constructed, many of the workers were housed there. We will now turn right and travel about 300 yards before we disembark."

His narration was timed precisely with the movement of the bus. When the bus stopped, a massive metal door in the middle of a dark green concrete wall appeared out of nowhere. A sign on the door stated in large red letters, "Danger High Voltage!"

"Move forward and to your right. Stand clear of the vehicle," the guide ordered.

"I feel like I should salute," Chelsea whispered and giggled.

Mr. Moore made a call on his cell phone and the massive door began to open very slowly with a groan. A security guard kept his hand on the door, as if he were guiding it until it stopped at a ninety-degree angle. The two men exchanged words and the security guard counted heads. He nodded and Mr. Moore signaled for us to follow him.

The group moved forward into the tunnel. It was well lit and wide enough for a semi-truck to enter. We walked about twenty-five feet, and Mr. Moore held up his hand for us to stop.

"Heads up," Mr. Moore announced and waited to get everyone's attention. "This former Government Relocation Facility was top secret during the Cold War. It was built between 1958 and 1961 to accommodate the U. S. Senate and the House of Representatives in the event of nuclear war. There were never plans to house the President within this facility. The

The Bunker Entrance

secrecy of this location was maintained for more than thirty years until *The Washington Post* published a story in May of 1992 exposing it."

"Who told?" Chelsea asked.

Mr. Moore gave her an annoyed look, but replied seriously, "The culprit was never apprehended. If you will hold your questions until the end of the tour, I would appreciate it. I plan to cover all the pertinent information while touring the facility."

"Sis," Brad mumbled. "He just told you to keep quiet. I think I like this guy."

"You mean the Little General," Chelsea mocked.

Mr. Moore walked backwards, facing the group as he continued to speak. "This protected substructure is buried 720 feet into the hillside. Ceiling and walls that are composed of three-feet of thick reinforced concrete surround it. There is also a 20-to 60-foot dirt cover between the substructure and the West Virginia Wing."

"I'm not so sure this was a good idea," I whispered to Chelsea

"Why?" Chelsea whispered back.

"Doesn't this give you the creeps? Like you're being buried underground?" I asked trying to muffle my voice.

Mr. Moore stopped walking and held up his hand. "Don't jump and don't scream. In about ten seconds the 25-ton blast door that you walked through when we entered the West Entrance is going to close." He folded

73

his fingers as he counted, "Steady now, five, four, three, two, one."

BAMMMMM!

Chelsea clutched her heart and gasped, "I do now."

"There you go again, acting like a drama queen," Brad scoffed.

"I'm not the only one," she snapped back after hearing several adults around us stifle screams.

Mr. Moore began to walk backwards again as he continued with the tour. "All four bunker entrances have doors and tunnels this wide, but not as long as this one. This tunnel is 433 feet long and slopes downward ninety feet. It provided a service area for rotation of supplies and materials. These circles to your right were large enough for trucks to turn around. Next, we are coming up to one of two decontamination areas. This is the smaller one."

He paused in front of a normal size doorway and a hall about four feet wide and six feet deep. Six showerheads were evenly spaced on both walls. He pointed to a chute on the right side of the wall just before the showerheads. "Keep in mind, this was a fallout shelter, not a bomb shelter. It was to be used in case of a nuclear attack. You disposed of your contaminated clothing here, showered with soap and water, entered the drying area to pick up new a set of fatigues or overalls, and then continued into the bunker."

Decontamination Chamber

A middle-aged woman asked, "Did the Congressmen and women send clothes ahead of time?"

Mr. Moore didn't scowl but answered the woman in a patronizing tone, "No, ma'am. Congress didn't know this place existed. The people in charge had clothing to personally fit every member of Congress, duplicate glasses or contact lenses for each, and an ample supply of each person's medication. For thirty years this area was constantly being restocked to meet the changing needs of all members of Congress."

74

From the decontamination area we moved into the power plant, the records room, the water treatment and storage area, the diesel fuel tanks, and the incinerator. The Little General gave statistics and explanations for all the equipment. My brain had clicked on "overload" thirty minutes ago. I wondered what Eric had thought of all this? Did he care about all these facts and numbers? I heard another group up ahead. I slipped into the hall but I didn't see Eric. I realized my group had entered a room on the right marked "Communication Center," so I quickly joined them. In this classroom size area, maps, digital clocks showing the time from major cities around the world, and a huge mural of the United States Capitol Building covered the walls. A large oak podium and a massive cherry desk were pushed against the mural. Theater-style seating filled the rest of the room.

Mr. Moore rested his arm on the podium and said, "You folks, take a seat and rest while I give you a brief history of the Greenbrier Resort. Nicholas Carpenter in 1749 settled this property by "corn rights," squatting on the land and farming it. His daughter Frances married Michael Bowyer in 1766 and laid claim to the property but did not reside here. Around 1778 the Anderson family brought their ailing mother to the sulphur springs to bathe and to drink the water. Within three months they claimed she was cured of rheumatic fever. Many settlers began to visit the area on a regular basis seeking cures. Mr. Bowyer, seeing a possible future as an innkeeper, moved his ten children along with two friends, a Mr. and Mrs. Wiley, onto the grounds. Two cabins and a stable were built on the property. As the number of visitors increased, Mr. Bowyer built a main tavern building and more cabins. After he died, the property was divided among four of his children. A daughter, Jane married James Caldwell from Baltimore. It was James Caldwell who had the springhouse built and the tavern expanded. From 1858 to 1922 the resort was called 'The Old White.' Before the Civil War at least eight presidents and Robert E. Lee visited on a regular basis."

I looked over at Chelsea and she was fast asleep. I nudged her and she bolted upright.

"Don't do that," she whispered.

"I didn't want you to miss the interesting part," I said.

Putting her hand in front of her face and trying to talk out of the side of her mouth, Chelsea commented, "Has he said anything about a horseshoe?"

I shook my head, no.

"Wake me when he does," she replied and let her body slide down in the chair.

Mr. Moore continued, "Other famous visitors included an Emperor of China, a Czar of Russia, a Sultan of Turkey, the Duke of Windsor, Prince Ranier and Princess Grace of Monaco, and Presidents Taft, Truman, Eisenhower, Kennedy, Johnson, and Bush."

"Wasn't this a prisoner of war camp?" asked a distinguished white-haired man.

"Yes sir," Mr. Moore said. "I was just coming to that. In 1910 the C&O Railroad purchased the Old White Hotel and began to build the new 250-room Greenbrier Resort. During World War II, 1942 to be exact, the Army took over the Greenbrier and used it to house German and Japanese diplomats. So I guess you could call that a POW camp. That lasted for about four months, and the resort reverted to being a five-star hotel. The Army came back again in a few months and this time bought the hotel for 3.2 million dollars. The hotel became Ashland Field Hospital. It remained an army hospital until 1946 when the army sold it back to the C&O. It cost approximately eleven million dollars to restore the Greenbrier to its present five-star status. Any other questions?"

As I looked around the room, I noticed everyone but Chelsea seemed interested in what Mr. Moore had been saying.

Mr. Moore ordered, "Then let's head'em up and move'em out. We have four areas left to visit."

The group began to rise and move toward the door. The elderly white-haired gentleman who asked about the POW camp had another question. "You never told us about the mural and the desk."

Almost snapping to attention, Mr. Moore answered, "I am sorry, sir. You are correct, sir. TV interviews were to be made from this room. With the Capitol in the background, a member of Congress could be behind a desk or podium and it would appear they were speaking from their office. A frame was added to the mural to make it look like a window, sir."

"They sure covered all the bases," Brad remarked as he shook Chelsea's shoulder. "Nap time is over. Let's go."

Mr. Moore led us down the hall and continued his lecture. "We will walk through one of the eighteen dormitories. Each dormitory (complete with showers, toilet facilities, and a small lounge) could sleep 60 people. One wall locker was provided for every two individuals, but each person had a metal drawer under his bunk bed to lock up any personal items."

We entered a lounge area for one of the dorms. A TV set, exercise bike,

76

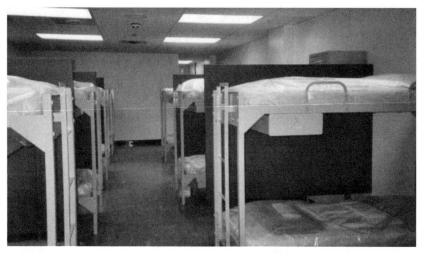

Dormitory

and seating for seven people were available. Our twenty-nine-member tour group crammed into the area.

"I guess all sixty never lounged at the same time," I said.

"Look at those bunk beds," Chelsea remarked staring through a doorway leading from the lounge.

"You are free to walk through the dorm. The toilet facilities are located in the rear. These facilities are used jointly with the other side of the dorm, which is identical to this side. Just follow through on your right. The corridor makes a complete circle back to the lounge," Mr. Moore explained.

I followed Chelsea as she led the way between the bunk beds. The center aisle was so small that we needed to turn sideways if someone passed. I was beginning to feel closed in; the walls seemed to inch slowly inward.

"Chelsea," I insisted, "move faster. I've got to get out of here."

"Look at these bunk beds," Chelsea said. "If you were to lie on your back, you would fill the whole bed. Gee, Brad would never fit. . . ."

"Yeah, yeah, whatever," I said urgently. "Come on, Chelsea, move faster. I don't like these cramped areas."

"Okay, Okay, I'm moving," responded Chelsea as she began to walk faster.

We walked through the group shower area, passed the sinks and private toilet facilities, and entered an adjoining bunkroom. It was a carbon copy of the one we had just left. It was here I passed Chelsea. I picked up the pace and dashed toward the hallway. Once I reached this less confining area, I exhaled. I could feel my heart pounding and my hands sweating. I took deep breaths and kept telling myself to calm down.

Brad came toward me in long strides. "Ginny, are you okay?" he asked.

"I didn't realize I was claustrophobic," I explained. "I've never had this happen before."

"You don't have to go into any of these rooms," Brad said.

"I know," I replied. "I'll be okay."

Brad and I stood to one side as the group following Mr. Moore moved down the hall and toward the clinic. I heard the guide explain that a twelve-bed ward, operating rooms, x-ray area, laboratory, intensive care unit, examining rooms, pharmacy, and reception area were located within this tunnel.

"Go ahead with the tour, Brad," I insisted. "I'll be fine. I'll catch up with you when they move to the cafeteria. That should be a larger area."

"Are you sure?" asked Brad. "I can. . . ."

Out of nowhere, Chelsea explained, "Of course she's sure. I just saw a sign down that hallway that said "Culinary School." That was the old bunker cafeteria, wasn't it?"

Brad replied, "According to the brochure it was. But I don't think the Little General will take it kindly if you two move away from the group."

Chelsea grinned and replied, "He's a big boy. I think he'll get over it. Come on, Ginny. Let's go."

Before I could answer, Chelsea had me by the arm and was leading me down the hall toward the Culinary School entrance. I looked back at Brad. He shrugged his shoulders, waved, and disappeared down the left corridor.

"We might even find a little snack," Chelsea hinted as we reached the double doors.

The doors opened into a brightly lit room large enough to hold at least 250 people. To the left was a huge island with three gas ranges and a wide stainless steel counter top. Mirrors were positioned overhead and behind this demonstration area, causing the light to shimmer off the metal surfaces. Three TV cameras anchored to dollies were focused on the ranges. A cafeteria-style serving station with a U-shaped tray rail stood apart from the cooking area.

"See anything to eat?" asked Chelsea as we moved toward the counter.

"Wow, is this place clean! How could you make anything to eat in a place like this? I'd be afraid I'd mess something up," I said.

"I guess whoever works here must feel the same way. I see no sign of any food. A mouse would starve to death in this place," Chelsea replied.

"There's something on the rail at the serving station, but it doesn't look like food," I commented as I moved in that direction.

"Probably a napkin," Chelsea guessed spotting the white square in the middle of the "U" shaped rail.

As I got closer I saw writing on the napkin. It was my name! It wasn't a napkin. It was a note.

"Chelsea," I squealed as I grabbed the note. "It's a note, to me."

My hands trembled as I opened the paper and read,

The hands of time will stand still,
If you seek a capital ideal—

Travel toward the mountain peaks, Across the
river bends. Missing treasures are easily found.
Allow help from strangers and friends. Respect
your heritage and mountain lore. Attempt to fine clues
left by me. Consider the notes and details.
Knowledge is the key.

"We're back to square one," Chelsea stated. "That's the same note that was left in the Cultural Center."

"Except for the *"hands of time,"* I corrected. "That part is new. But who ever heard of time standing still?"

"Do you think there is a gray truck outside," Chelsea asked as she looked around the room.

"Oh, for Pete's sake, get serious. Do you always have to be looking for some guy?" I said glowering at Chelsea.

"Look, California, don't you yell at me. It just seems every time we find a note, some dude in a gray truck is around. And, for your information, I'm not always looking for a guy," she angrily snapped at me.

The double doors opened, and Mr. Moore was again walking backwards and saying, "The cafeteria was designed to feed 400 people at one seating. The kitchen kept a 60-day supply of food at all times. The entire cafeteria/kitchen area covered more than 7,500 feet, making it ideal for todays usage-the Culinary School. The school moved into this area in 1995, and is open to the public. The general population, since 1962, has also used the last three rooms that we will visit. They just didn't realize they were in the bunker. Follow me into the Exhibit Hall and the meeting rooms."

The minute Brad spotted us standing near the serving station, he moved toward us. I waved the note in the air as Chelsea pointed to it.

"Where did you find it?" Brad asked as he reached for the note.

"In the bend of the serving rail. It's like a modern tubular-shaped horseshoe," I said, watching Brad's expression as he read the note.

"It must be in Charleston," he muttered. "But I'm not sure about this *"hands of time"* stuff."

"Come on," Chelsea ordered. "Let's get out of here and head for Charleston."

"How?" Brad asked. "The car is in White Sulphur Springs. We have to finish the tour and ride the bus back."

"Oh, no," groaned Chelsea. "That could take hours."

"Maybe not," I answered looking at my watch. "When we left, the Little General said the tour would last approximately two and a half hours. We should have only about thirty minutes left."

"Then let's catch up with the group and try to keep anyone from asking a question," suggested Chelsea.

We hurried to fill the space behind the tour group. We listened impatiently as Mr. Moore explained that thousands of guests had used the Exhibit Hall for various functions throughout the years. Originally, it was designated to be the workspace for Congressional support staff members to conduct the business of government. It was large enough to hold twenty-four offices and ninety computer terminals. The East Tunnel entrance, like the West Tunnel entrance, was a vehicular passageway. It had a 30-ton blast door at one end and an 18-ton concealed door leading onto the second floor of the Greenbrier Resort. This interior entrance was well hidden and sported a bamboo motif. From the second floor of the resort, we walked back into the Exhibit Hall and moved deeper into the bunker. We entered the two present-day theaters named the Mountaineer Room and the Governor's Hall. The Mountaineer Room was for the Senate to meet and the Governor's Hall was large enough for the House of Representatives. Phone jacks, installed on every third seat for Congressional business, remained on many seats. Since this ended the tour, we began to retrace out steps to exit.

Chelsea, Brad, and I moved to the front of the group behind Mr. Moore. Luckily, he seemed as anxious as we were to be leaving. We hurried through the long corridors without glancing into the rooms we had visited earlier. When we reached the interior entrance to the West Tunnel, Mr. Moore came to an abrupt stop. He made a quick call on his cell phone and motioned for us to follow him once again. The guard at the far end of the tunnel began to open the door when we came into view. I saw the bus waiting for us outside. My heart began to beat rapidly in anticipation of finding the golden horseshoe.

The bus ride back to the Civic Center was short and uneventful. We exited the bus and dashed toward the car.

"Buckle up," shouted Brad as he jumped behind the wheel. "Let's go to Charleston."

FACTS

1. The Indians began the salt industry on the Kanawha River near Malden. They set up boiling pots, evaporated the water, and recovered the remaining salt. Mary Ingles, captured by an Indian war party at Draper's Meadow, Virginia, in 1755, became the first white woman known to have used this method.

2. Lewisburg is the county seat of Greenbrier County and one of the oldest towns in West Virginia. In 1774, General Andrew Lewis, for whom the town is named, gathered his forces here at Camp Union before the Battle of Point Pleasant. The town was chartered in 1782 by the Virginia Assembly and prospered as a way station on the James River and Kanawha Turnpike. Camp Union was later called Fort Savannah.

3. Lewisburg has been designated a 236-acre National Register Historic District by the National Trust for Historic Preservation. More than 60 structures and the site of a Civil War battle contribute to the National Register Historic District.

4. John Withrow House/ General Lewis Inn is a hotel located on 301 East Washington Street. The site of the hotel is on ground that formed part of the Confederate line in the Battle of Lewisburg in 1862. Withrow, a Confederate officer, hid for several days in a secret room in the attic when Federal troops came looking for him. To prevent looting by the soldiers, the family stored wheat beneath the stair treads and silverware under the front portico steps.

5. The Old Stone Presbyterian Church on 200 Church Street was built in 1796 of limestone. This is the oldest church west of the Alleghenies that has remained in continuous use.

6. The John Wesley Methodist Church on 209 East Foster Street was constructed in1820 of handmade bricks. During the Battle of Lewisburg, May 23, 1862, a cannonball struck the southwest corner of the church.

7. The present-day Greenbrier County Library was erected in 1834 by James Frazier, as a library and study for the Court of

Appeals. A section of old plaster, where soldiers scratched their names during the Civil War, is still visible.

8. Historical information about the Greenbrier Resort and the former Government Relocation Facility (bunker) is as stated within this chapter.

Chapter 7

One Search Ends

"How could we be so stupid?" Brad exclaimed. "Of course it would be in Charleston. No one in his right mind would take such a valuable item so far from the Cultural Center. We have wasted all of this time. . . ."

"It's too simple," I protested. "All of the other clues had hidden meanings. Why would this one be so obvious?"

"Maybe it's already been found," responded Chelsea, "and this clue was just to bring us back to Charleston."

"Keep trying to get Sakura, please. Maybe she can get to the Capitol and find it before someone else. Gee, do I ever feel stupid."

I kept insisting, "There's something not right here. I can't put my finger on it, but I have a strange feeling that we're missing something."

The ringing cell phone startled Chelsea. She grabbed it and turned it on. "Hello," she said. "Oh, Sakura, we've been trying to get you. We found a note. . . . You too. . . . You're kidding, that's what our note says."

"What, what, what?" Brad said impatiently glancing at Chelsea and trying to watch the road at the same time.

Chelsea replied, "They found the same note, but not at the Greenbrier. Their note was on the windshield of her Jeep, parked at the Civic Center in White Sulphur Springs. They feel as dumb as we do. They won't meet us in Beckley. They're on their way to Charleston."

Brad said, "Tell them to start searching. We'll get there as soon as we can."

Chelsea relayed the message and then listened intently. She covered the mouthpiece of the phone with her hand and asked, "Sakura wants to know if we have any ideas about where to look in the Capitol." She looked at Brad and then at me.

I shrugged my shoulders and replied, "I'm blank."

84

Brad knitted his brow, and mumbled, *"The hands of time. . . ."* in or on some clock, maybe? Right now, I can't think of anything in particular. Tell her we'll keep thinking about it, and we'll call if we can come up with something."

Chelsea delivered the message, said good-bye, and placed the phone in the holder on the dashboard. She leaned back in her seat to think and closed her eyes. Brad looked lost in a trance as he drove cautiously on I-64 toward Beckley. I gazed first at the note and then at the lush green mountains. The word capital kept running through my mind like a chant. I was seeing the word letter-by-letter, c-a-p-i-t-a-l . . . . a-l. That was it! I looked at the note again and with a pencil circled the capital letters:

Travel toward the mountain peaks, Across the river bends. Missing treasures are easily found. Allow help from strangers and friends. Respect your heritage and mountain lore. Attempt to find clues left by me. Consider the notes and details. Knowledge is the key.

"Tamarack!" I screamed as I bounced up and down on the seat. "It's at Tamarack!"

Brad looked at me through the rearview mirror. Chelsea turned in her seat and took the note.

"Capital, with an "al" is not a building. Here it means capital letters. Look, it spells out Tamarack," I said joyously.

Brad looked toward Chelsea as she confirmed, "It does spell Tamarack with the capital letters."

Brad remarked, "The seat of government where the legislature meets is spelled c-a-p-i-t-o-l; that much is right. What about the other clues? *"Toward mountain peaks. . . . "*

Chelsea interrupted, "The orange jagged roof at Tamarack is suppose to represent the mountain peaks."

"Your *"heritage"* is revealed in the crafts and foods they sell," I added. "Remember all the advertisements. Tamarack was described as the art and soul of West Virginia. It was built by West Virginians, for West Virginians, to exhibit the best of everything from the entire state. It's got to be there."

"Okay," Brad muttered in deep thought, *"knowledge"* is represented by the books. All the books are about West Virginia or written by West Virginians. There's a lot of folk *"lore"* in those books, but where does *"rest and good food"* come in?"

"Duh," said Chelsea slapping her forehead. "It's a rest stop for tourists and the Greenbrier does the catering. This is beginning to make sense."

"Around the river's bend" is the one I don't get," I admitted.

"I know that one, " Brad piped in. "It's close to the New River, and coming from the airport you need to cross Bender's Bridge."

"Bender's Bridge," I mumbled. "I remember now. That's where we saw the gray truck."

Chelsea's eyes grew large, "The truck again. . . . you're right, Ginny. It's got to be Tamarack. I'd better call Sakura."

Chelsea reached for the phone as Brad suggested, "Run all these ideas by her. See if she, Morgan, and Erik agree with us."

Chelsea explained our thinking to Sakura and waited for her to pass these new ideas to Erik and Morgan. Chelsea listened carefully and then asked me, "What about *"the hands of time?"* How does that fit with Tamarack?"

"I don't know," I responded. "How does it match with the Capitol?"

After some thought Brad offered, "Tamarack exhibits the *"heritage"* of West Virginia at the present time in a futuristic setting. It's all about time."

Chelsea rolled her eyes as she repeated my question and Brad's explanation over the phone. She waited for a response and then added, "We'll keep working on it, too. See you as soon as possible. Bye."

"Are they coming back to Tamarack?" Brad asked.

"Yes," said Chelsea. "Erik loved your idea, Ginny. He said to tell you that you're the smartest girl he knows."

I felt myself blush as I thought of Erik. I was looking forward to seeing him at Tamarack, but I was also filled with dread. If we found the horseshoe, would I ever see him again? I was glad Brad and Sakura were an item. That should help all of us stay in touch. I tried to get Erik out of my head and focus on *"the hands of time."* What did it mean?

"There's a sign. Five more miles and we're there," said Chelsea.

I was so excited I was leaning between the bucket seats. The *"hands of time"* kept running through my head. Maybe, using their hands they buried a time capsule. Would we be allowed to dig it up? No, that couldn't be right. A time capsule wasn't buried in late May or the first of June. Surely, we would have heard about that.

Brad turned left onto a bridge that crossed all four lanes of the West Virginia Turnpike. I could see Tamarack above the service area. The or-

Tamarack

ange sculpted peaks looked like a sunburst high on top of the mountain.

Brad turned into the upper visitors' parking lot and we scurried out of the van. We ran toward the building, dodging travelers as they ambled along the wide walk discussing their purchases. The shrubbery and grass were neatly trimmed around the stone and brick walkways. Ivy clung to the wall near the cornerstone proclaiming Tamarack as the Caperton Center. We entered through two enormous glass doors. Straight ahead were two smiling women behind a reception desk covered with tourist brochures. The glass wall behind the desk revealed an inner courtyard dotted with metal and ceramic sculptures.

"May I help you?" asked the older woman looking over the rim of her glasses.

Brad quickly moved toward her and answered, "Yes ma'am. We're one of the teams searching for the golden horseshoe, and we have reason to believe it is somewhere in this building."

"You and many others," she replied. "We've had four teams to come in during the last few days. In fact, one of those groups may still be in the building."

"Has anyone found it?" Chelsea questioned.

"Not that I'm aware of," she answered.

"Do you know anything that might help us?" I inquired.

She sighed and said, "If I knew, I would turn it in for the reward."

Brad said politely, "Thank you. We'll just look around for a while."

"Enjoy," she said, turning to greet another group of tourists approaching the desk.

We moved away from the desk and to the right. "I don't know where to start looking. All we can do at this point is walk through the area and look for anything that might be about the *"hands of time,"* explained Brad.

"Ginny, you check out the clothes. Brad, you look in the Gov. Hulett C. Smith Theater. I'll take the jewelry department. Hey, they might have some watches—*"hands of time,"* get it, " said Chelsea.

I nodded and walked toward the colorful clothing. Multi-colored garments flowed from hangers and counters. Dresses, capes, scarves, mittens, and sweaters felt soft and cozy to touch, as I randomly moved in the midst of fabrics rarely seen in California. The style of casual country living clothes trickled into uptown city attire. There was everything from painted canvas tennis shoes to evening wraps and glitzy accessories. I saw many items with Tamarack's logo, but nothing of a golden horseshoe. I noticed that Brad and Chelsea were standing in front of the David L. Dickirson Fine Arts Gallery, and I moved to join them.

"Nothing," I shrugged.

"Ditto," said Chelsea. "There were lots of watches with hands, but no golden horseshoe."

"I checked every row of seats in the theater and the stage. It was clean," Brad remarked. "Let's check out the prints inside the art gallery."

The three of us entered the gallery and headed in different directions. I wandered among floral watercolors and admired the pastel swirls of the artist's brush. I read the title, name of artist, and any other information about each painting. I even checked around the floor and in the corner. Nothing. The expanse of the glass wall caught my eye again as I noticed the courtyard and its landscaping. The paintings blended nicely with the natural beauty of the outdoors.

Chelsea, Brad, and I met just outside the art gallery and continued our circular search of Tamarack. The Greenbrier Grill on the right was filled with delightful aromas and hungry diners. Their coffee shop on the left sold the trademark rhododendron china, handmade candy, and sportswear emblazoned with the springhouse logo. A display of hand-carved dulci-mers with CDs in the background lay ahead. As we moved into this area, I became aware of the music piped throughout the center. It seemed to be a mixture of Irish and Celtic folk songs played on dulcimers, violins, and banjos. Handcrafted wooden furniture was placed in strategic positions along the circular aisle. Rocking chairs of all shapes and sizes, deacon benches, and Adirondack chairs provided a place to rest and a view of numerous crafts.

"This would be my favorite place," I announced to Chelsea as I gestured toward several decorated Christmas trees.

"There are lots of ornaments up there," said Brad.

"Yeah," replied Chelsea, "and if we're lucky, one of them might be a horseshoe."

"You really think so?" I questioned. "If it were openly displayed, I think someone would have found it by now."

Brad answered, "I don't know what to think anymore. Let's keep looking. Maybe the other groups missed it."

Brad moved toward the left to examine the Christmas trees and ornaments more closely. Chelsea and I scanned rag dolls, marbles, wooden toys, and coal figurines on the right. We then maneuvered through a large area of wooden utensils featuring trays, canes, candlestick holders, cutting boards, bowls, and even a dining room table with six chairs. No sign of the horseshoe.

"Nothing," I sighed. I turned toward the center courtyard and gazed at the massive pots of red geraniums placed to enhance the shape of a large metal sculpture in the middle of the outdoor area. A single humming bird flitted around the geranium at the base of the sculpture and two white butterflies fluttered near the top. I looked at the metal and tried to figure out what it represented. It appeared tall and straight with a triangular arm reaching from the top to the middle. It reminded me of the protractor I used in geometry class. My eyes followed the shadow of the arm to the circular base. The base was marked in twelve sections like the face of a clock. A clock, the *"hands of time"*!

"Chelsea, Brad," I screamed running toward the glass doors opening to the courtyard. "I've found it! It's outside."

I reached the sundial and panted with excitement. Brad and Chelsea joined me with looks of amazement on their faces. I dropped to my knees and began examining the base of the sculpture. *"Hands of time,"* it's a clock," I explained.

Chelsea and Brad stared at me in disbelief as I fell to my knees and began searching the twists and crevices of the sculpture. I felt every bend of the cold metal and scratched in the cedar chips around its base. Nothing. Why weren't they helping? They just stood there. I felt like crying.

"Ginny, it's a sundial. There are no hands," Chelsea said putting her arm around my shoulder. "But it was a good idea," she added.

"Yeah, you're thinking along the right track," agreed Brad. "We need a break. Let's go in and get a bite to eat. Sakura and company should be here soon."

I moved toward the glass doors, dragging my feet. I really felt stupid. I was glad Eric wasn't here to see me fall all over that sundial. The horseshoe had to be here, but where? We entered the building and turned toward the Greenbrier Grill.

"Wait, I see Sakura coming up the walk with Morgan and Eric. Let's see if they want to eat with us," suggested Brad as he led us across the floor toward the entrance.

"Tamarack, Tamarack," Morgan bubbled almost dancing through the entrance. "Why couldn't we see it sooner?"

Eric smiled and gave me a hug, "Beauty and brains, you've got both, Ginny."

I blushed and replied, "But we haven't found the horseshoe. Maybe the capital letters in the verse were a hoax. Other groups have also searched here and. . . ."

"Wait a minute," Chelsea ordered. "Look out there! It's the gray truck. The maniac. He's got to be around here somewhere. Let's go find him. I've had enough of this appearing and disappearing act."

"Every time we see that truck, a note appears," Sakura remarked.

"He's got to know something," exclaimed Morgan.

"You're right. He's got to be a major player," Eric responded.

Tapping Eric on the arm, Brad said, "Let's roll."

The two guys began running toward the front doors. We followed them out and onto the walk. Sakura, Morgan, Chelsea, and I paused just outside the front doors and watched a tall, lean young man dressed in denim and wearing a black cowboy hat step onto the running board of the gray truck. He turned, removed his hat, and waved it at us. The sun glazed his blonde curly hair.

"The hands, the hands," he shouted pointing his hat toward us. He jumped into the truck and started the motor just as Brad and Eric reached it.

Brad jumped on the running board and grasped the mirror on the passenger's side of the truck. Eric reached for the tailgate but couldn't hold his grip. As the truck made a sharp left turn, Brad was thrown to the ground.

"Oh, no" cried Sakura as she rushed down the long walk. When she reached Brad, he was dusting himself off and trying to act cool. She threw her arms around his neck and began to cry softly.

"I think I'm going to be sick," Chelsea moaned. "Look at that. He just loves it."

Morgan replied, "I think this might be serious."

I wanted to rush out and meet Eric, but the golden horseshoe was on my mind. Right in front of me was a bronze plaque containing cornerstone information. This plaque was bordered in hands. Six, eight, twelve, thirteen, my heart was beating fast as I counted.

"Chelsea, Morgan," I shouted tugging on their arms. "Look, hands!"

"Hands," Morgan shouted jumping up and down.

Eric rushed up the walk as Chelsea and I hugged each other. "All right," he shouted.

The four of us moved closer and began to scrutinize the hands. A single hand held each corner of the brass marker in place. Four sets of hands were evenly placed around the marker, one set on each side. In three of these sets the hands were clasped, but in the top set they were about six inches apart. A thirteenth hand rested alone near the top left corner.

"Are these the *"hands of time?"* I asked.

"They're hands; that's for sure," Chelsea said.

Morgan added, "They're all different. Some have cuffs around them, some are bare, some belong to women and others belong to men."

"Why would they put hands around a cornerstone?" Sakura questioned.

"They probably represent the people of West Virginia," explained Brad. "You know, the builders of the state, craftsmen, writers, miners. . . . all the people of the state."

"Look, in the right hand," I gasped pointing to the pair of open hands at the top of the cornerstone. "A pouch."

My hand was trembling as I reached up and plucked the small bag from its resting place. I lowered it and untied the gold cord. From the weight and shape of the pouch I knew the missing horseshoe would be inside. I picked up the lower corner of the bag between my thumb and index finger causing the horseshoe to slip smoothly into my palm. It was beautiful. The gold shimmered in the sunlight, and the sapphires and diamonds emitted flickering sparks of light. For a moment I was breathless as I closed my fingers around the icon. I could feel warmth and energy tingling in my hand. This was the same magic I felt last summer as I traveled back in time. It was real. Excited voices and jostling bodies brought me back to reality.

Chelsea remarked, "Hey, California, remember us. We want to see too."

I opened and extended my hand to "oohs" and "aahs" as my cousins and friends reached for the golden horseshoe. It was passed gingerly from hand to hand. A crowd began to gather around us and strangers were patting us on the back and offering congratulations. One of the ladies from the reception desk came over to inform us she had called the governor's office. We were to remain at Tamarack until a representative from the Cultural Museum and a State Trooper arrived.

"Now I'm really hungry," said Brad. "Ginny, you hold on to the horseshoe and let's celebrate. Come on; I'm paying."

Brad handed me the horseshoe with one hand and slipped his other arm around Sakura's shoulder. He led the six of us toward the grill. Morgan and Chelsea followed the happy couple while Eric waited for me to put the horseshoe back in the pouch. After tying the bag securely and placing it in an inside zipped compartment of my backpack, we joined the foursome.

"We're going to be rich. I just know it," Chelsea sputtered.

"How much is the reward?" asked Morgan.

"I don't know, but something this valuable must be worth lots," Chelsea answered.

"But this horseshoe belongs to your government, your state," remarked Sakura. Should you expect a reward for returning property that is not yours?"

"You don't understand," Morgan began.

"A reward was offered," Chelsea interrupted. "If we hadn't found it, someone could have made a lot of money by selling it."

"But they didn't sell it," Eric injected. "They left it in a very protected place and gave clues to people willing to search for it. They made it interesting and fun."

"Too easy. Something weird is going on. That's for sure," said Brad with a confused expression.

"Are you saying it was never stolen?" I asked Eric.

Silence swooped down and covered the group of six as we ate mechanically. Now that the day's discovery was questioned, the celebration suddenly became gloomy. No one reached to sample another's food and glasses were never refilled. Confusion and weariness crashed the party.

"Ginny, Ginny," said Eric nudging my elbow. "I think they want you."

I looked up to see two men standing behind Brad. The State Trooper stood at ease while the short man in the brown suit was staring at me.

"Oh, I'm sorry," I sputtered. "Did you say something?"

"Yes, I did. I'm Jared Wright with the state department and this is Trooper Bellamy. We're here to take possession of the missing horseshoe. I believe you have it," said the man in the brown suit.

"Yes," I replied pulling my backpack onto my lap. I felt all eyes on me as I rummaged in the zipped compartment in order to produce the horseshoe. I firmly clasped the treasure and handed it to Mr. Wright.

"Please, remove it from the pouch," requested Mr. Wright.

I loosened the cord and slid the horseshoe into my palm. I passed the horseshoe to Mr. Wright and proceeded to slip the velvet pouch into my pocket. It felt stiff for some reason. I hadn't noticed that before.

Mr. Wright and Trooper Bellamy examined the horseshoe. They mumbled and nodded as they turned the icon from side to side.

With a smile on his face Mr. Wright announced, "You've found it! This is the real thing. Congratulations!"

The six of us cheered as Mr. Wright shook our hands. Trooper Bellamy wrapped the horseshoe in tissue paper and placed it inside a metal box with a combination lock.

"Hey," Chelsea shouted, "how about the reward?"

"That will be presented to you later at a special ceremony in the Governor's mansion. My secretary will be getting in touch with all of you to make the necessary arrangements," Mr. Wright replied.

"Can you tell us how much it is?" Morgan asked.

"That will depend on how much you use it." Trooper Bellamy said with a smile on his face.

"What do you mean," I asked.

The policeman replied, "Didn't you know? It's two nights room and board in every state park in West Virginia over the next two years. That's for all six of you. If you go to only a few parks, it won't be much, but if you go to all the parks, that could be quite a bit of money."

"All right," Eric shouted.

"I'll be happy with that," Brad said, smiling with Sakura.

"Ginny," said Chelsea, "that's means you will be back here for the next two summers."

"And maybe holidays," added Morgan.

"I'm happy with that," said Eric taking my hand underneath the table.

"I'll be here," I replied.

Mr. Wright and Trooper Bellamy said their good-byes after getting everyone's name, address, and phone number. We gathered our belongings and started to leave the grill. Eric took my hand when we left.

"Ginny," he said, "I'm really glad you're coming back."

"Me too," I replied giving his hand an extra squeeze.

"This summer isn't over," Eric continued. "Maybe Sakura will bring us down next week, or we could meet somewhere."

"I hope so," I said.

Brad pulled the van next to us and said, "Time to go, Ginny. We have a couple of hours ahead of us."

Eric moved closer and bent his head toward mine. Chelsea opened the door just as he brushed my cheek with his lips. It was a kiss, not on the lips, but still a kiss. I climbed into the van, closed the door and blew him a kiss through the window. I couldn't wait until next week.

Once inside the van, Chelsea said, "He's cute, Ginny. I think he likes you, too."

I blushed and replied, "I hope so."

As I tilted the seat back and stretched my legs, I realized the pouch was still in my right pocket. I pulled the soft bag out, opened the cord and turned the sack inside out. A folded slip of paper dropped onto the floor. "Chelsea" was written on the front of the paper.

"Chelsea, look, it's for you," I stammered handing her the paper.

"For me! You're kidding. Who? Well, how?" she gasped taking the note. She read the note silently and then handed it back to me.

I read aloud:

I'm looking forward to seeing you next summer. You pick the park and I'll be there.

Gray Truck Driver

95

About the Author

Frances B. Gunter retired after thirty-one years of teaching school in Cabell County. During this time she received numerous awards. The Daughters of the American Revolution chose her as Cabell County American History Teacher of the Year in 1986 and won the state award for American History Teacher of the Year in 1987. In 1989 she was recognized by Phi Delta Kappa of Marshall University for outstanding leadership and was presented the Phil M. Conley Award for exceptional service to the Golden Horseshoe Program. She represented Cabell County public schools as Teacher of the Year 1990-1991 and was presented the West Virginia State Reading Council's Citation of Merit Award for *The Golden Horseshoe I*. Her family participates and encourages her writing. Her husband, Ron, travels with her throughout the state collecting information and taking pictures. Daughters, Vivian and Ronda, assist in proofreading and adding personal anecdotes.